CALL OF THE TRAVELER

MORE BOOKS BY TONI BINNS

<u>Nexus Universe - Traveler Series</u>

- Traveler Forgotten (*Short Story*) - Available at tonibinns.com
- Choice of the Traveler
- Call of the Traveler
- Courage of the Traveler

CALL OF THE TRAVELER

TRAVELER
BOOK TWO

TONI BINNS

BARDHWOOD PRESS, LLC

Published by Bardhwood Press, LLC, Shelton, WA

Paperback ISBN: 979-8-9853073-1-3

Library of Congress Control Number: 2023908142

To all those called to serve, be it family, friends, or cause. To help others is true nobility.

CHAPTER

ONE

This damn book.

Betha stared at the cover, wishing she could just get rid of it. She had taken to carrying the scrapbook from her mother in her bag. The therapist she had seen since the funeral didn't think it was odd but that it might be part of her healing process. While she was glad Grandpappy had found a therapist for both her and Angie, she was frustrated at how little progress she seemed to have made and wished she could feel better more quickly.

The sound of the coffee shop was relaxing. That was why she sat inside. That and the fact that her favorite table was outside in the drizzly rain. The warm fall was turning to winter. Snow would come soon, and no matter how warm her hoodie was, she would need to switch to a heavier jacket.

The rain couldn't wash away the destruction in town or across campus. Betha shook her head and tried to push those thoughts away. Thinking about the battle wasn't a good thing. She wasn't ready for that. Just ignoring the horror of the struggle wasn't the best strategy, but it worked most of the time.

"Vanilla latte, right?" asked a familiar voice.

Betha's head snapped away from the window. Susan from her economics class was holding out a mug. "Yeah, I'd love another one," Betha said. Her thoughts focused on what had happened and how Susan had helped. "But I guess you knew that, right?"

Susan blushed and motioned to the chair. "Can I take a seat? We should chat."

"That sounds ominous, but then again, what's the worst that can happen?" muttered Betha.

Susan set the full coffee mug next to Betha's empty one and took the empty chair. "You shouldn't tempt the goddesses of fate like that. They seem to have a weird sense of humor."

"That's true," Betha replied, thinking of her own junior year so far.

"I wanted to apologize for deceiving you when we met on your first day," said Susan. "I knew we had to meet for that conversation to happen. Otherwise, worse things were going to happen." Susan gave her a soft smile, but her fingers kept fiddling with her to-go cup.

Betha tried to remember what Susan was talking about, but then it hit her. Susan had mentioned she should get her Traveler's mark checked out at the medical center on campus. That comment from Susan had sent her to the med center where she'd discovered she was a Traveler. Everything else followed from there.

If that hadn't happened, then she wouldn't have been at the nightclub and Kyra wouldn't have been nearby. Dots connected inside her head.

"Holy smokes. It all stemmed from that. You knew?" Betha leaned back in her chair, barely breathing. That one moment had changed everything. That was terrifying.

"Sorry, I am not that awesome. All I knew was that was the best way for you to be introduced to what you were. Not the rest of it. I am not all-knowing." Susan shook her head and took a sip of her own coffee. "Believe me, I wish I had seen more of that, but yeah, that's not how it works." That was a weird way to phrase it. Betha wondered how much of the demons' invasion Susan had seen. It sounded like not much.

"How does it work, being what you are?" asked Betha. Eric had mentioned that no one knew what Susan was, and it was important that no one found out. Betha hadn't realized that seers were in such high demand, only that the seer for the council was gone, and they were looking for a new one. Yet Susan was adamant that no one outside of Betha and her Anchors find out that she was a seer.

"It's frustrating and incomplete. I'm always working on pieces of information and trying to figure out things on my own. If I could give it up, I would. No one should know what I know." Susan squeezed her cup and then let her hand relax. She took a deep breath, then continued. "So yeah, I am sorry that I couldn't just come out and tell you."

Betha nodded. It was like Susan had read her mind.

Betha empathized with feeling like she didn't have enough data to make good decisions, and she was always learning something after the fact. No matter what she did, she was always operating on not enough info. But unlike Susan, Betha wouldn't give up what she was. She was supposed to be a Traveler—it was what she was meant to do. She could feel it in her bones.

"I get it, and I forgive you," said Betha. "You helped us at the end there, and we appreciated it." Susan had called Eric and warned them about the trap the prince had set. It had given Betha time to come up with a plan.

"You had that in the bag. The concern was making sure that all of you made it back..." The idea Susan had seen not all of them surviving the encounter with the prince was scary. Yet she couldn't let her mind go down that rabbit hole. They were all here and safe. "But speaking of helping you out, you should ask Kyra if you can go to the next council meeting. It's important." Susan took a sip of her coffee after dropping that statement.

"Demons-invading-important?" asked Betha, slightly holding her breath. She wasn't sure if she could take on another invasion right now. Part of her felt fragile. Very fragile.

Susan wiggled her nose. "Similar but different. I can't really give you more than that."

Betha sipped her latte. It was perfect. She trusted Susan. In class, she asked excellent questions, and she helped everyone out with studying. "That has to suck, that you can't say everything." Betha was glad that she was not a seer.

Susan set her coffee cup down slowly. "It really does, though in this case, I really don't know. I feel like one wrong move and anything bad that happens is on me." Her words came out quickly like she had unintentionally said more than she wanted. Susan slid her chair back and stood. "I better get going." She glanced out the door and then back at Betha. "I don't know if this will be helpful, but Eric shouldn't go on your next trip."

Betha opened her mouth to reply but Susan held up a hand. "I don't even know what it's about, but if he isn't here, things get weird, here on Terra. Not the-world-is-going-to-end weird, but something gets pushed off...I don't know how else to explain it."

"Good to know." Betha did not know what that meant. Things get pushed off—pushed off from what? How does someone even try to wrap their mind around that?

"I wish I could be more helpful, but I need to run." Susan tried to smile at Betha, but it was only half-hearted. She quickly headed out the door into the rain. Betha wondered what she was fleeing from.

Betha leaned back in her chair. A glowing presence in her mind moved closer. She couldn't help the smile that took over her face. Her best friend entered the warm shop with Joey. They were holding hands, and Betha wanted to swoon. The two of them looked so cute together. It was a great distraction from the churning mess in her mind. She wanted what they had. Not that she needed a boyfriend, but she wanted someone to hold her hand and pull her close.

"Do you need a refill?" asked Angie through their bond, snapping Betha out of her thoughts.

"Nope, Susan got me one...."

Angie turned and looked over her shoulder at her, eyebrow raised.

"Don't interrupt your date for this!" Betha scolded her friend.

Joey turned to see what Angie was looking at. He caught sight of Betha, and a giant grin came over his face. He said something to Angie that Betha couldn't catch, given the background noise in the shop, and headed her way.

"Betha! My second favorite person!" He held his arms out, and she climbed to her feet for the hug he was aiming for. Joey hugged her extra tight. His hugs were the best hugs. Better than his doggie kisses, anyway.

"Isn't your second favorite person Ben?" asked Betha.

Joey pulled away and took a seat at her table. "Ben is ranked lower than normal. He is talking about staying up north." Joey leaned in closer over the table. "Personally, I think he found a lady bear. It still feels weird that he hasn't come down to check on us."

Betha understood Joey's point, but then again, the war they had fought had changed them all. At least Joey didn't seem to limp anymore. Hopefully Ben would show up and Joey would get some answers.

"Speaking of lady friends... You and Angie, huh?" she asked.

Joey's smile grew softer. "You can't trap me with that. I know that you already know all about us, but to answer your question: Yes, and I still can't believe it." He glanced down at his hands. "I have always loved her, but given the differences between us, I never thought it would be possible. The clock was always ticking until she was going to be drafted and sent to do who- knows- what." He glanced back at Angie with a soft look in his eyes. "Now we have a fighting chance, and my goal is to get it right."

Angie approached the table with a snarky grin. She set down two to-go cups, and the smell of chocolate wafted toward Betha.

"Are we staying or going, Joey?" asked Angie.

"Well, my dearest Betha, it is time for me to go. Don't study too hard," said Joey, glancing down at the book.

Betha gave him the go-away motion. "Go you two—I need to finish this up."

Joey grabbed Angie's free hand as they headed out of the coffee shop, and Angie blushed. Betha loved every moment of watching them. If Joey and Angie could work, maybe she and Carter could work.

The two of them headed out and Betha reinforced the walls she had created in her mind. It kept her emotions from flowing into the others, and right now that was important. She didn't know how Angie had so much control, and Carter and Eric seemed to just not care. She wanted control over when and how her emotions and thoughts were shared, and it was hard. She was working on it though.

She flipped through a couple more pages of the scrapbook, but nothing caught her attention. Betha took a deep breath and pulled out her phone. She quickly texted Kyra before she lost her nerve, asking to go to the next council meeting.

The reply came quicker than expected. "That's funny, I was going to invite you to come, you just barely beat me to it. See you on Thursday at 2 p.m."

ANGIE WASN'T sure what to think. Neither the cold rain nor Joey's hand could distract her from wondering what Susan had wanted. The last time the seer had gotten involved, the world was ending, or it had at least felt like it. Dread trickled along her spine. All of that fighting had taken a toll on both her and Betha.

Therapy was helping, but the idea that another battle was on the horizon scared her.

Joey's fingers tightened on hers. "I don't know where your thoughts went, but we are here. In the rain. With hot chocolate."

Her eyes snapped to his, and she couldn't help but let her shoulders relax. They were heading to the movies for an afternoon matinee.

"You're right. Also, it is raining a little bit more than anticipated," she replied.

Joey let go of her hand and wrapped his arm around her waist. "That just means we are getting a little damp. The hot chocolate was a good idea for the walk."

The social center on campus had a small movie theater, and it was showing some feel-good love story. Joey had jumped at the chance to ask her, so here they were. "I do come up with some good ideas," Angie said, with a touch of playful defensiveness.

"Of course you do. You are awesome," Joey responded automatically, with the simple, matter-of-fact tone that said this was a truth of the universe.

Angie blushed at the compliment. She turned to reply, and he caught her lips with his own. It was a soft kiss that quickly deepened. Tasting him was always an adventure, and it was still so new. Joey slowly pulled back. Never did she think this was possible. Somehow, she would pay Betha back for the joy this brought.

"You are going to dump all of your hot chocolate if you aren't careful," he whispered.

Angie realized she had gotten so caught up that she had ignored the to-go cup in her hand. Hot chocolate dribbled down the side and over her fingers. "I might have some left," she said sheepishly.

Joey took the cup with one hand and lifted her fingers to his mouth with the other. He playfully licked the chocolate up. Heat ran up her body and Angie couldn't think straight. Joey let go of her fingers with a grin. He still had her drink.

"Wait, what happened to your cup?" she asked.

Joey blushed bright red and shrugged. "I got distracted and dropped it."

She glanced down and saw that his cup had crashed to the walkway at some point. Hot chocolate was all over the cobblestone near their feet. The rain was slowly washing it away. Angie couldn't help but laugh. He picked up the cup to toss it in the nearby trash can.

"You totally just stole my hot chocolate."

"Maybe?" his reply came, complete with the puppy dog eyes that got him in so much trouble.

His laughter joined hers. Angie knew whatever was coming, she would face it. Moments like these were too important.

"Angel fire is pulling power from your core. It feels like a sun in your chest that you pull from as needed," said Eric. He held a hand over the area, which was also right where their Anchor tattoos had formed from Betha. Eric could feel the ball of energy in his chest, right under his hand. Physically it wasn't there, but mentally that was where he pulled from.

The air was brisk, but the sky was still clear. The trees surrounding the clearing had lost their leaves, but the pine trees were still a deep green. In a few weeks, the weather would switch to rain mixed with wet snow, then finally just snow. For now, though, it was nice enough to be practicing outside. This clearing was hidden from view—you either needed to fly or walk through the forest to get here. It was safe from prying eyes.

Eric could tell Carter listened to him, but he just couldn't reach him. It felt like Carter was holding back, but Eric had never known his brother to hide from anything. It didn't make sense. Eric even connected with his brother through the bond, so he could feel what he was doing, yet success seemed out of reach. The ball of the sun was there, sitting on top of Carter's chest. When Eric did connect with his brother, it was like the ball of light was filled with lead. It seemed so heavy. Eric had no idea how he was keeping his shoulders straight or his head held up high. His own shoulders hunched over in response to the pull.

"Just poke at it," suggested Eric. He flashed his brother a goofy smile, one he'd always used in their childhood just before they would get into trouble.

Carter rolled his eyes. "That doesn't do anything," he growled.

Eric held up a hand. "I am only trying to help. Don't get angry. You remember what I used to do as a kid when I got angry?" That was an understatement. When he had been angry or frustrated, after he manifested, angel fire would come out to play. They had gone through multiple copies of the same board games that he would lose at. Burned to a crisp, every time, and Eric wasn't fireproof. Carter was trying to learn to summon angel fire now, but they didn't need to accidentally scorch the whole forest.

A winged shadow flew overhead and landed in the clearing. Carter's shoulders tensed up and he turned away from the figure. "You deal with him. I just need a break." Carter turned toward the trees and walked away from Kellion. Eric stared at Carter's back, but knew he wasn't going to change his brother's mind. This was so much harder than he'd thought possible.

"Does he still not want to talk?" asked Kellion softly. He kept his tone just loud enough for Eric to hear, without Carter overhearing. The distance between them had increased, but Carter had stopped walking. Instead, he stood there like a brat. Being in between his brother and his grandfather was definitely getting old for Eric. The wind was a little chilly, but Eric ignored it.

"He is so angry," answered Eric. "I don't know what you said to him, but he wants nothing to do with you."

Kellion's wings vanished, and he twisted his hands together. The sign of worry looked out of place on the normally perfect calm of the angel. "I misjudged the situation and assumed that he would be overjoyed that he had manifested. It did not go well."

"So, why are you here then? He isn't going to take any help from you anytime soon." Even if Carter needed it. Learning from Eric wasn't working, no matter how much he wanted to help his brother. They just couldn't connect. And Eric couldn't figure it out.

Kellion's eyes stayed on Carter. "The angels have arrived," he said, just loud enough to carry. Carter turned back toward the two of them.

"What does that mean?" asked Eric. The angels never just showed up. Usually, a message arrived beforehand, and it was a big deal. Parties were thrown. Everyone in Haven went all out with decorating, along with trying to hook up various bloodlines. Matchmaking at its finest. It was such a dog-and-pony show. A few years ago, he would have thought it was awesome. Lots of women to flirt with. But now it felt like he was on display. His eyes were also opened a little bit more since his anchoring with Betha, and Eric wondered what the catch was with the gatherings. No one was encouraged to settle down, but date around. He didn't understand the end game.

"You didn't think that Traveler Betha going to the heavens wasn't going to have consequences, did you?" Kellion asked.

Eric rolled his eyes. "You are the one who asked her to go. This lands on your shoulders." He motioned toward the sky. "You can deal with their bullshit."

"It isn't that simple." Kellion motioned toward Carter. "They are going to want to know about him."

"I manifested, isn't that what everyone has always wanted?" muttered Carter, turning back toward the two of them. "Isn't this what you and Father wanted?" It seemed someone still wanted to be part of the conversation. He didn't need to yell across the clearing; he could have just stayed where he'd been when Kellion showed up.

Kellion let out a sigh. "I only ever wanted you to be safe and happy. He is returning."

"Who?" asked Eric.

"Your father."

Angel fire erupted across the area, scorching the air. Before Eric could move, Kellion dashed forward, creating a barrier. It contained the molten white light. Suddenly, the flames went out.

Carter was on his knees surrounded by blackened grass. It stretched several feet in each direction. His body shook and Eric moved forward, kneeling next to him. Well, at least something had gotten a reaction from his brother. That cinderblock on his chest felt lighter, ever so slightly. Eric held out his hand to his twin.

"Well, you poked it all right," commented Eric. A weak chuckle came out of Carter, who reached for the outstretched hand. "Now if only you could do that when you wanted to."

"I'll get there," said Carter, pulling himself to his feet with Eric's help. "It will just take practice."

"He will want to see you both..." said Kellion, trailing off. Eric brushed the grass off his pants.

"I don't care what he wants. We are anchored and he has no rights. The angels don't have rights over any of their offspring born on Terra," said Carter. "The Accords state as much."

"You know better than that. I'd think you would want to see him on your terms rather than deal with an ambush."

Carter shook his head and his wings shimmered into view. "I can't listen to this right now." He jumped up and his wings spread as he took to the air. Both angels on the ground cringed as they watched. Carter flew up erratically and barely got enough height to keep above the trees.

"At least he is flying now," commented Eric. It had taken a week for Carter to be able to pull his wings out and put them away. He hoped Carter would make it back to the main part of campus without an incident.

"His emotions are all over the place," said Kellion. "He needs to get that under control."

"Grandfather, he hasn't even been an angel for two months. Let him be!"

"He has always been an angel," replied Kellion. "His blood just wasn't activated."

"What does that mean?" demanded Eric.

"Watch out for Carter—try to distract your father. It feels like everything is balancing on edge. I don't want either of you falling." Kellion shook his head as he, too, jumped to the sky. Eric stared after, wondering how he was going to keep on top of it all.

THE ONE THING everyone gathered for was training. It was an unspoken rule that everyone showed up on time. It was early, but it was also the only time they could reserve the open gym on campus just for them. It was way more space than they needed to practice, but they learned the hard way just to reserve it. Otherwise, they had folks watching them, and that made Betha nervous. Exercise machines and lifting equipment took up half the space. The rest was an open area with a very thin mat on the floor for sparring, sword fighting, or group exercises. It had a light smell of sweat no matter the time of day.

Betha still felt uncertainty with her Anchors. Each was different in their own way, but she hoped they all viewed this as a chosen family. Regardless, they were stuck together, till death do they part. They had all fought together—won and survived—but things had changed. It seemed they were in this weird, awkward space now that they weren't fighting just to live through each day.

Eric preferred to focus on sword combat, and he was leading today's session. While Betha wasn't an expert, she was getting better. The muscle memory she seemed to get from Carter was a lifesaver, and everyone agreed she was further along in her combat skills than she should be. Angie was facing off against Eric, and she was facing Carter.

Betha blocked the strike from Carter, and he gave her a smile. Since Carter had gotten wings, he could move faster and hit harder. It made fighting against him much more difficult. "I know you dislike fighting, but defense is important." He swung his saber at her, and Betha dodged. She couldn't argue that.

"I know," she replied. She swung out with her own weapon, but he easily blocked the blade. Her problem wasn't knowledge, it was lack of desire. Images of striking down the demon prince haunted her. Taking his life was necessary, but she hated that she'd done it.

"*You can hate what you did, and it can be the right thing at the same time,*" sent Carter through the bond. Betha missed blocking his blade and dove for the floor.

"*I know,*" she replied. Her temper rose, and she tried to keep the walls in place in her mind. Carter reached out to help her up and she ignored it. "I got this." She did not need another lecture. As it was, this was something everyone wanted to talk about, and she just wanted to leave it alone.

"*You good?*" asked Angie silently.

Her temper jumped up again, and she swung out at Carter. Her anger rippled, and fire traveled down the blade. Carter blocked with his sword, which flickered in return. Bright white light washed over the room, then went out. Carter pulled his blade back as Betha's lowered.

"Shit," whispered Betha. She hadn't meant to do that. Angel fire wasn't something to play around with. It could burn through almost anything if you could sustain it long enough.

"I think you mean *awesome*!" commented Angie from across the room.

"Well, Betha can use angel fire like Carter," said Eric.

Carter continued to look at her without saying anything.

"If only I had meant for that to happen," added Betha. At least she was honest about it.

Eric walked closer. "It happens to all of us. You are learning, just like Carter."

"I think I need to cool down," answered Betha. She slid her sword into her scabbard and headed toward the door that led to the courtyard. Carter quickly followed. She could hear his footsteps behind her.

"Well, her speed is up," added Angie.

"Just like your speed. She is pulling more from each of us," answered Eric, "especially him."

She was outside before anyone could comment further.

THE DARK PRE-DAWN sky didn't show any stars. That was the first thing Betha looked for whenever she was out at night—the stars. But tonight, clouds hinted that rain might start at any moment. The sudden chilly air caused goosebumps to rise on her arms, and she rubbed them, staring at the trees. It was down that path in the distance that the prince had opened a portal on campus after she had left. She had walked out of the in-between there. It was hard to think about, and she knew she needed more time to process everything that had happened.

"Are you okay?" asked Carter.

Betha had ignored the fact that he had followed her out into the early morning air, but now she couldn't.

"I don't know how to define okay," said Betha. "I am coping the best I can."

Carter stepped up next to her. "I think that's all that we can do right now."

All she wanted to do was lean on him, but she still didn't know where they metaphorically stood. Ignoring him was easier. "I didn't mean to get angry. Just dealing with becoming a Traveler, all of the demon stuff, and my mom dying. It's a lot."

Carter wrapped his arm around her side, and she leaned in. Tears sprang to her eyes, and she wished they would vanish.

"No one cares that you got angry or used angel fire. We get it. Believe me, I get it." Carter looked down at her, and she couldn't help but look back up at him. His blue eyes seemed to stare into her soul. One moment she was angry, then sad, and now she was distracted. Betha couldn't look away—she didn't want to. "Everything shifted for you rather suddenly, and dealing with it is hard. I understand. It is going to take time for you to find your feet. Just let me know if I can help. I want to be here for you."

A buzzing sound came from his pocket before Betha could respond. Then he pulled away. "We only have fifteen minutes left in the gym. We better pick up after ourselves."

Carter stepped away and headed back inside the gym. It took a moment, but Betha realized he could have been talking about himself as well. Maybe he was struggling just as much as she was.

CHAPTER

THREE

Betha jumped at the knock on her door. She had been engrossed in the studying materials she had to get through for her marketing class. The case study was all about how to design products and services to fit customer needs. It seemed more like psychology as opposed to marketing. While her therapist had thought she should take more time before going back to classes, Betha had decided she needed to be doing something. She still felt so behind compared to her peers.

Betha could feel Angie approaching, but she wasn't close enough to be the one who had knocked. Betha took a deep breath to calm herself, then climbed to her feet to see who was here. When she opened the door, her best friend was just down the hall, but no one else was in sight. There was, however, a box sitting at her feet.

"Looks like you got something," said Angie as she approached. "What did you order?"

Betha shook her head and picked the box up. "It wasn't me. I haven't had a chance to even think about shopping. It's from some company called Magical Emporium of Wares?" The box was plain except for her address and the name of the shop in a rather fancy script. It seemed to glow light gold.

Angie whistled as she joined Betha inside her room. "That's a fancy place. I wonder who it's from."

Once the door was shut, Betha tore into the box like a kid at Christmas. She loved getting gifts and surprises since they had been so infrequent growing up. She quickly removed the tissue paper, revealing a soft pair of leather boots. They looked like her size. She twisted them around, but there wasn't a tag inside. The boots looked custom-made.

"Those are amazing. You have to try them on!" gushed Angie.

"I will, give me a moment." Betha set the boots down, then searched the box for a card and found a small envelope. It was better to be safe than sorry. It wouldn't do to miss the card because she was too excited for the boots.

I hope you find these useful. They have a concealed pocket
- Carter

"He *has* to like you," replied Angie once Betha handed over the card. Betha quickly removed her sneakers and slid her feet into the boots. Somehow, they fit perfectly. They went up to her knees. "I wonder what the..." Betha's voice trailed off as she darted into the bathroom. She pulled down the shelf on top of the large towel rack. Betha removed the knife taped to the back of it.

It took a few minutes for her to recognize, but the

right boot felt different. It had a place to slide the knife inside, hiding it from view.

"That's just brilliant," whispered Angie. "You can't even tell. It's better than the shoulder strap you were using."

Betha switched over to mind-speak. She knew shifters could hear over long distances, and she didn't want anyone else knowing she had the knife. Speaking within the bond had gotten easier, and everyone's control had increased, even though sometimes things still leaked when someone was excited or worried. "*Yeah, no one knows I still have it. Kyra can only guess. I told her it was destroyed in the in-between. Now I can keep it on me, safe and sound.*"

Angie responded out loud. "Well, those had to be expensive. Have you tried to ask him out again?"

Betha paced around her room to test out the boots. "I almost did this morning, but I bailed. To be honest, I think we are both dealing with a ton of changes in our lives, and we have plenty of time to figure it out."

"That's totally why you didn't ask him out." Angie gave her a pointed look, and Betha could feel her cheeks heat up. Her friend knew she had chickened out. "Did you at least mention the council meeting?"

"Slipped my mind. Plus, the two of us can handle it. Right?" Betha took a seat next to Angie at the table.

"I mean, we should be fine, but I thought we weren't going to keep secrets from each other?" asked Angie.

"It really isn't a secret, but I get what you are saying."

Betha reached out to both Eric and Carter via mind-speak. "*I am going to the council meeting this week at 2:00 p.m. Susan recommended it, and Kyra was going to invite me anyway.*"

Eric replied first. "*You spoke to Susan? Shit, what'd she say?*"

Betha quickly recapped the conversation, including the remark about Eric staying behind "this time." Everyone was quiet after that. They all agreed that listening to her warning last time had saved their asses, so they wanted to heed her current warning as well. If they didn't listen to her and things went sideways, it would be on them.

Carter finally responded. "*We don't know what it could mean. Just need to make sure we don't jump to conclusions. Kellion mentioned something about angels visiting, so it could involve that. We will know on Thursday, either way.*"

Betha didn't like the sound of that. Visiting the angelic world had been a giant pain. While she had gone to get support from the angels, it had actually turned out to be the path to get the knife. Yet, that empty, bright white space still haunted her. She had thought she was going to die, but she hadn't. They had been victorious. Together, they would get through this as well.

Betha didn't know what to expect as she was ushered up a set of stairs and onto a balcony. The guard who showed her the way vanished after Betha, Carter, and Angie were shown to the balcony seats. Betha glanced around the small space before plopping down in a chair. It felt like they were at a theater performance. The seats were wooden and free standing, but the balcony railing in front of them felt weird, not like a movie theater where the view was clear. Then again, she hadn't ever been to a live show before, so maybe this was normal. More alcoves wrapped around the room at the same level that they were on. They all looked down below at a central platform with a large table that was surrounded by chairs. Rings of additional seats were set on the floor, looking up at the central table. The chatter from below was a little loud, but Betha did her best to ignore it.

"So this is the council," stated Betha. It felt like they were underground, but she had seen the building from the outside, so she knew they were in a large hall. There was no outside light, however. It seemed strange, again reminding her of a theater.

Angie took up a position near the curtains blocking the seating area from the hallway. Carter sat down next to her. Betha realized she had missed a podium at the far end of the table, toward the northern end of the room.

"Yes. Every species and major political group has someone here or has opted out," answered Carter. He motioned to the balconies surrounding them. "Most in the upper regions are folks who don't attend often or are visitors. The big table hosts the more significant power groups on Terra." So far, only a troll was seated at the main table, along with what she assumed was someone who was an elf. It was hard to tell from far away.

"It's headed by a human, right?" asked Betha. The general council stuff had been part of her civics class her first year, so it wasn't particularly fresh. She could have done a quick rundown before coming, but cramming was not her strong suit.

Carter nodded. "It is."

More and more people filtered into the seats below, and the noise grew softer. Betha recognized Justin, who headed Angie's Pack, as he took a seat at the table. Others moved into place, leaving three chairs empty.

"One of the empty seats is where Andrea sat. She was the old seer. She died during the demon attack. The fey are one of the others, and usually don't attend. It looks like Kellion is also missing." Carter's voice was soft at the end of the sentence, and Betha resisted asking how things were going between the two of them.

"You would think you couldn't miss a meeting," muttered Betha. The fact that someone would just opt out of their duty didn't sit well with her. The council head called the meeting to order, and soon Betha grew bored. The only human didn't seem unique in any way, and his voice droned on. She wasn't sure why Susan and Kyra wanted her here. The various representatives presented long, boring reports on rebuilding after the demon attacks. Betha knew as well as anyone how much work was still needed, and the reports didn't seem to add much.

"Our last order of business is to let the council know that a host of angels have arrived on Terra. They are hosting a recruiting drive for pilgrims to enter their realm. This is one of their options as stated in the Accords. We have Guards making sure that they follow the rules set forth by the charter."

A rush of whispers rose up, and Betha noticed that

Carter gripped his armrest tightly. The council head concluded the meeting, and the people at the table exited together.

"What does that mean?" asked Betha. "I could barely survive there—how can they invite pilgrims?"

"It's complicated." Carter's voice came out through clenched teeth, and it was clear he'd had no idea this was happening. His voice rolled across her mind. *I'll tell you more about it later. Every so often, they do this. It's how my brother and I were conceived.*

"Wait, you mean they are here to have sex with people?" her mind shouted. Thankfully she responded in turn, through the link, though she realized after the fact it went to Angie and Eric as well. Angie cleared her throat and Betha noticed the Guard was back.

"All of you have been invited to the private session of the war council. Please follow me." He quickly led the way down a hallway and staircase to a different area of the building. Guards stood flanking the door, and Betha realized that the doorway was different. It was like a ripple. Angie had taken her through one on her first visit to the Nexus.

Now that she knew it was different, she realized what it did—it created a door in a stone wall where one wasn't. She bet that Kyra could close it and shut the room down. The Guard motioned for them to go through the ripple, and Betha went first.

Inside was a spacious room with a table smack in the center. Twelve chairs surrounded the table, and most were already full. Her eyes locked on Kyra, who motioned her over. Betha could feel several people staring at her as she made her way around. Justin gave her a nod as she passed by.

"You can sit here." Kyra said as she pulled out the chair next to her for Betha to sit down. Angie and Carter took up a post standing against the wall behind the two Travelers.

Betha glanced around the table, doing her best to not stare at everyone who glanced her way. She recognized the troll from the table in the council room, and Justin, but that was it. The troll caught her eye and gave her a solemn nod, flashing his horns, which were painted bright blue.

The council head entered the room and took the chair at the head of the table.

"Our guests should be here shortly. Once they are inside, you should lock up," the council head said. The last comment was directed toward her, but she realized it was meant for Kyra.

Kyra nodded and motioned to Betha beside her. "For those who don't know, this is Betha. She is the new Traveler." Several folks nodded their heads, and Betha caught sight of elven ears and a smile from a vampire. There was one person who looked human.

"That's the head of the witches' coven," whispered Carter in her head. *"I don't know her name, but the vampire's name is Vincent. The elf is Devon."* Betha could feel Eric nearby, but she couldn't pinpoint him. He had stayed behind, so it was strange. It was like the ripple that was the door was disorienting her senses outside of the room.

"Son, it is good to see you!" The voice echoed in the empty hallway in the basement of the council hall. This was the hidden entrance used to mask the arrival of special guests who did not want the attention of the full council and their many attendants. Approaching footsteps echoed against the cool, stone floor and Eric turned toward the sound.

A tall angel with bright white wings wrapped him into a hug. He held Eric close for a moment before letting him go. His eyes glowed a deep blue, and he did not look old enough to have a son Eric's age. "Father has told me of several of your deeds during the demon invasion here. You did well."

"Thank you, Father." Eric gave him a head bow before smiling brightly.

"I heard your brother finally manifested. It shows good things for our bloodline that both of my sons are angelic. Twins, and the heritage showed. I couldn't ask for more."

That wasn't exactly what had happened, but Kellion didn't do anything without reason. If their father shouldn't know about how Carter manifested into an angel, they would keep their mouths shut. Eric kept his face steady, and he glanced up as Kellion joined them quietly from an open doorway along with another person who Eric couldn't identify. Kellion was the one who had asked him to show up as a favor. Now his grandfather gave him a glance that he couldn't decipher. The stranger wasn't an angel. Instead, he had wings like a bat. It wasn't the first time that he wished he had been a more diligent student.

"Hopefully, you can convince your Traveler to fix the issues we are facing," said his father. Kellion took the lead, directing them down an empty hallway.

"My Traveler?" asked Eric.

"Yes, I heard you both are anchored—attached." His father kept his eyes ahead. "I'd rather you both procreate rather than become attached, but such things can still happen. We need to keep the bloodlines fresh."

"Fresh?" Eric felt like he was repeating everything his father said. This wasn't making sense.

"A quarter angel makes the transition to our world easily. It's when it's diluted more that we have issues." Eric felt Kellion tap his shoulder. Maybe he should stop asking questions. Yet his father continued without prompting. "We need to bring another round of pilgrims over and spread the bloodlines while we're here. There are several families that we need to increase the angel blood power in. That's not a conversation for here or now though. First, we need the Traveler."

The doorway ahead was flanked by two Guards, and Eric could sense that Betha and the others were on the other side. He reached out to them, trying to keep his face blank.

"Incoming. Father doesn't know the truth about Carter's manifestation. This visit has something to do with Betha," he sent through the bond.

～

CARTER FROZE next to the wall. He hadn't realized that their father was going to be at this meeting. It should have dawned on him that he would be leading the delegation to Terra. After all, the last time he was here, he had conceived twin boys. That had brought so much honor to the family.

Carter took a deep breath and tried to steady his feelings. The fact that his father wanted Betha for something made his blood boil. But losing control here would be a disaster.

Kellion entered the door and smiled at the table. His eyes locked with Carter's, then they flickered to Betha in her seat before he announced, "Lord Seth of the mighty eighth host from the angelic realm, along with Sir Samson from Sky World."

Next to enter was Carter and Eric's father, his wings displayed out behind him. Each feather glowed bright white with angel fire. His eyes seemed to glow a deep blue, then all of the light vanished, along with his wings.

"Freaking angels," muttered Carter.

Then a gray figure entered. He had black hair with dark eyes. His only clothing was a pair of leather shorts. Sir Samson had wings, and a pendant dangled against his chest. Carter's lips parted in shock once he realized what he was. *"Holy shit—gargoyle!"* echoed along the bond. Carter's shock vanished as he realized the gargoyle, who must be Sir Samson, was staring at Betha. Sir Samson's eyes peered at her like she was the only light in the darkness.

～

BETHA WASN'T IMPRESSED with the twins' father. She could feel Carter's emotions toward him along the bond, and they weren't pleasant. The light and dramatic entrance were wasted on her. It was like a peacock flashing his feathers. Quick glances down the table showed her that everyone was likewise bored with the display.

Yet, the next person to enter was a different story. Betha felt Kyra stiffen next to her. Sir Samson immediately looked at Betha. His gray eyes met her hazel eyes, and she knew that there was something special about him. She could almost feel him on her radar. It wasn't like he was her Anchor, more like her power recognized what he was. What the heck was going on?

CHAPTER

FOUR

"Welcome Lord Seth and Sir Samson. We are the High War Council of Terra. Please take a seat." The head of the council motioned to two chairs at the foot of the table, opposite himself, that stood empty. Lord Seth took a chair while Sir Samson remained standing. His gaze had left Betha, but his eyes kept flicking back to her as if he couldn't believe it.

"You have come to petition the High War Council, and we are excited to hear you," continued the council head.

"Not exactly," started Lord Seth. "As you know, I am here to oversee the pilgrimage for anyone of angelic blood who wishes to relocate to our realm. I am also here on behalf of our allies, the gargoyles. Sky World is not affiliated with Terra or the Accords. They do not have a direct connection to Terra but are connected to the angelic realm and the High Deserts which connect in turn to the Fey Wilds."

Lord Seth motioned to Sir Samson. "Sir Samson is a

High Warrior of Sky World. We have had an alliance with Sky World for several millennia. They are dear to our light. They called on us several years ago to help with a demonic invasion." It seemed everyone on the council went still as one. Betha's breathing stopped. Again with the demons.

"Breathe, Betha," came a whisper through her mind from Carter. She realized she could feel that Angie was on edge, along with Eric. Carter seemed to be the only one who wasn't anxious. Instead, he had a ball of anger spinning in his chest. It flicked into Betha's mind. She could see it clear as day, then it was gone.

"It has come to our attention that you also had a situation with the demons. You called on us and, unfortunately, we were on lockdown dealing with an ongoing demonic invasion in Sky World. All of the Heavenly Hosts apologize that we could not come in time to aid the Council. The Eighth Host assembled as soon as we realized that you weren't reporting the same invasion that we were already dealing with. Though it seems you were successful in the time it took for us to arrive. We applaud your success at defeating the demons and slaughtering the demon prince."

Sir Samson's gaze flicked back to Betha, and he opened his mouth several times. He kept tapping his fingers on his side.

Lord Seth motioned Kellion forward. "To apologize for our unfortunate timing, we have prepared a gift for the council, and one for the bounty on the demon prince." Seemingly out of nowhere, Kellion withdrew a large crate and thumped it down loudly on the large conference table. "Twelve of our blades forged in angel fire to help hunt down any remaining demons is our gift for the council to use in its wisdom. For the bounty on the Prince of Hell—"

"Sky World is dying," Sir Samson cut in and stepped forward. His voice shook, and his words rang out loud in the chamber. "Even with the angel's help, we—my people—are dying. They are falling from the skies, wings broken. Hoards keep coming." His eyes went to Betha, and he banged his fist on the table. "Hidden rifts bring more demons whenever we push back." Samson reached into a satchel to pull something out. Angie tensed, ready to pull Betha out of danger, but Samson slowed his movements. He set an object carefully on the table. It looked like a scrap of dark leather, but it had a hardened point.

Bile rose in Betha's throat as she realized it was a wing from a child, a gargoyle child. "They send back the wings. Our....Littles..." His voice broke, then gained strength. "Starwalker, we need your help. We cannot hold onto our world for much longer. Please, help us."

Lord Seth's lips pressed tightly together, and he glared at Sir Samson. He barked something in a language that Betha didn't know. Sir Samson carefully picked up the wing and then stepped back.

"I apologize for Sir Samson's outburst. As you might imagine, he is managing a difficult situation," said Lord Seth.

"I'll do it," answered Betha. "I will help Sir Samson."

"Betha, we don't know anything about him!" sent Angie.

"That's a child's wing, Angie—can you really say no?" replied Betha. She could feel her friend's hesitation.

Kyra grabbed her hand. "We can discuss Traveler Betha heading your way in a few days."

"My thanks, Starwalker," replied Sir Samson. His eyes were watery, and he turned away from the table.

"Well, this has been an intense conversation. Let's break for a brief intermission," said the council head. He pushed back his chair and stood. Several people followed.

The troll stood up and excitedly slammed his giant hands on the table. "My people will escort the little Traveler to Sky World. It is our turn to protect her." He motioned toward Sir Samson. "We of the Endless Fields remember our cousins of Sky World. We pushed the demons out of Terra, and we will push them out of Sky World."

"Garruk, it's break time," answered the head.

"I am Garruk, the Axe that Cleaves in Two. We will not be denied in helping our cousins. This is a blood debt!" His voice came out as a growl.

"I am not stopping you, only asking to table this discussion for fifteen minutes."

"Have your fifteen minutes. It will change nothing," said Garruk. He turned immediately toward Sir Samson and marched over.

Betha pushed back her chair and quickly followed Angie out of the room. She could feel Carter right behind her.

"Carter, my son," Seth said as Carter passed.

"Not now," answered Carter in a firm tone, not even hesitating as he continued to follow Betha.

Vincent headed out of the room, and Betha quickly followed him and Angie through the weird door. He stepped aside and watched her pass, a smirk on his face. His eyes glowed in the hallway light.

Angie kept moving down the hall, so Betha followed. Her breathing picked up as the image of the wing on the table cut across her mind. They made a sudden turn into an empty room. Angie pulled her into her arms.

"Breathe, it will be okay," whispered Angie.

"Fucking demons... children!"

"I know, I know," her friend said. Angie rubbed her back.

"We will figure this out," said Carter. "We support you."

Someone joined them in the room, and Betha pulled away from Angie. Eric gave her a soft smile. "I guess I missed something important." He hadn't been in the room—he didn't know.

"I volunteered to go help the Gargoyles with their demon portal problem." Susan's suggestion of Eric not going on the next trip came to mind. "They are ripping wings off children." Betha's voice broke, and angry tears streamed down her face. They took her mother, and it still wasn't over with. Why would someone do this?

"Well fuck, Susan was right, I guess there's another quest," answered Eric.

Carter gave his brother a nod. "I'll go check to see if Betha is needed in the meeting after this."

THEY HAD BEEN DISMISSED, but Carter had stayed behind. He had mentioned that Kyra wanted to meet with Betha tomorrow. Betha, Angie, and Eric had decided to head back to campus. The ride back to the dorms was quiet. Betha was wrapped up too much in her own thoughts to hold a conversation.

"Let's head up to my room. There is more space there," said Angie as they parked.

Once they were all sitting in her room, Eric started, "I guess Susan doesn't think I should go..." his voice trailed off, then he added. "And it doesn't sound like the angels are leaving anytime soon."

"One moment," interrupted Angie. She grabbed her phone and ordered some pizzas and a salad. "Food is always needed to make a plan."

Betha curled up on the couch with Angie. She nodded to her friend, then replied to Eric, "Yes, she thinks you should stay behind. No offense, but your dad seems to be a dick."

Eric chuckled. "I mean, he is. Most angels are. Kellion is the nicest one I've even heard about, and I am not just saying that since he is my grandfather. It was why there were no hurt feelings within the angelic ranks when he chose to stay on Terra to be the angels' representative on the council. He was such an oddity. Since then, Lord Seth has been a perfect example of what an angel should be and has since redeemed the family's name."

"So you are supposed to be like him? Lord Seth?" asked Betha. "Showing off and always in charge?"

"I mean, he would prefer it. Especially now that Carter has manifested."

"What was up with that situation?" asked Angie.

"No idea. We are going to have to corner Kellion to find out what is going on and why Father doesn't know about what happened when Betha came back from the angelic realm. He only mentioned that Carter had manifested, but not how." Eric paused, then continued. "Kellion also came to warn Carter and me about Lord Seth while we were training." He summarized the conversation they had in the forest.

"That is concerning," said Angie. "And I thought the Pack had issues."

"Yeah, Susan's warning..." Betha let her words trail off.

Eric nodded. "I agree, I should stay here on Terra. It leaves you three to watch out for each other. I can try to figure out what the angels are doing here. The conversation with my Father on the way here was strange. I felt like he thought I knew something important, but I didn't."

"Don't forget, Garruk, the Axe that Cleaves in Two," added Angie.

"What?" asked Eric.

"The troll on the council said he would go and protect me," said Betha. "I don't really understand it. Something about a blood debt to their cousins the gargoyles."

Angie's phone rang, and she smiled. "I am going to go grab the pizzas from the front desk." She squeezed

Betha's arm, then headed out, leaving Betha and Eric alone.

"Are you okay staying behind?" asked Betha. "I know you and Carter are close."

"We have been around each other more since we have been anchored than in past few years. And this feels important."

"Not to mention you might run into Susan," said Betha. To her surprise, Eric's mouth opened, and nothing came out. "She blushed a bit mentioning your name. There might be something there."

The door opened, and Angie walked in empty-handed. "You aren't going to believe who tried to steal our pizzas."

Joey came in red-handed, carrying a stack four pizzas tall, plus an order of garlic knots. "Guilty as charged. They smell way too good—I couldn't help myself." He set them on the coffee table. Betha couldn't help but smile at Joey, yet it faded a bit. This time, more than her was going to be leaving Terra. Including Angie, just when she and Joey were figuring out what they could be.

"So what horrible thing is happening now?" asked Joey. Everyone turned toward him in surprise. "Angie ordered garlic knots—those are the big guns. I can keep my mouth shut. That's why I grabbed the pizzas." Three sets of eyes flickered to Betha as he continued, "I know I am not an Anchor, but I am a friend."

Betha patted the couch next to her. "I don't think any less of you because you aren't an Anchor."

Joey took a seat. "Don't worry, I am not fishing to be one either. I prefer to be boring Joey. It took some time for me to realize it, but I am not a fighter. I spent a lot of time talking with Ben, you know, and there's something to the way bears approach things. They don't fight unless they have to, though they'll protect their own when threatened. I'm kinda like that. I will attack if I need to, but I don't want to. You know, with my fierce barking and jumping about."

Relief flowed through both Angie and Betha. Turns out they both didn't want Joey to be an Anchor. He was a good friend, but she agreed with his assessment.

"I get that," said Betha. "No, the bad news is that the demons weren't only attacking Terra, and there is another world that is in trouble."

"Shit—that's bad. You'll need to go help them."

"We are," replied Betha. "We are going to help them. Eric is going to stay here, but Angie and Carter are going with me."

"That's good. They can watch out for you." Joey's eyes grew wide. "Not that you aren't kick-ass, Betha. Just, you aren't a fighter either."

Leave it to Joey to sum her up in so few words, but it was her problem with all of this. She hated to fight, and she hated hurting anyone. Even demons. She didn't know how to respond.

"When are you leaving?" asked Joey. Betha glanced up and saw that he was looking at Angie.

"We aren't sure yet. It will be soon, maybe two or three days," answered Angie. "It's pretty bad, like geno-cide bad."

"Oh."

"Yeah."

"At least we have pizza tonight, and pack." Joey motioned around the room. Betha smiled. They were a pack, a chosen family. Add in Carter and Grandpappy, and this was all she had left. Looking around, though, it was enough.

Betha headed to the coffee shop. Kyra was going to be meeting her nearby and since she was on campus she was thankfully alone. Last night she had crashed at Angie's along with Joey, who slept in his lab form. It was the most sleep she had gotten in weeks. But even though she loved her chosen family, it was nice to have a moment to herself to process everything that had happened in the last day or so.

There was a pep in her step, but she blamed the boots for that. They fit perfectly, and each time she saw them, she wanted to go talk to Carter. He hadn't shown up last night but had let them know that the council meeting had gone on late. At least it was a warm day, and her thick sweater was enough with the sunshine.

"Hey Betha," called out Kyra. Betha spotted her sitting at a picnic table near the coffee shop. "I grabbed you a latte—the barista said it was your favorite." She motioned to the to-go cup sitting on the table. The coffee was a nice gesture, but for some reason, the hair on the back of her neck went up.

"Thanks. This might be one of the last days where I can just hang out and be outside," Betha said as she walked up and took the coffee cup.

"I love these rare fall days," said Kyra. "They remind me of home and the celebrations we would have for our holidays. In mid-winter, we would have a large gathering celebrating the darkness and then the return of the light. It is a lot like the solstice celebrations here." Kyra smiled brightly, and her gaze settled off in the distance. "The coffee isn't the only gift I bring." She reached into her coat pocket and set a box on the table. It was slim but long and made of some sort of wood. "It is the bounty on the prince."

"I am not sure I want it, whatever it is," answered Betha. "I don't feel like I deserve a reward for killing, even him."

Kyra shrugged. "I swore to give it to you, so I am." She slid it across the table. "It is rare as heck, so don't go tossing it away."

Betha picked it up and realized it opened like a case for sunglasses. The wood didn't make a sound as she cracked it open. Inside lay a bright white feather that seemed to shimmer gold and silver in the sunlight.

"A feather, really?" Her eyebrows rose as she stared at Kyra.

"That's a feather from an archangel. Don't lose it." Kyra motioned her to close the box.

"Archangels? You mean like Michael and Gabriel?"

"Exactly like that. That's from Michael. Actually, *the*

Michael. Archangel of Justice. I guess many angels have tried to take down any demons from the royal family. The archangels honor those who succeed with a feather."

Betha's stomach flipped over. They killed demons for feathers. "I don't think I can keep this." She reached out quickly to Carter. *"I just got a feather from Michael the archangel for killing the Prince."*

"Don't lose that. We will talk more later," replied Carter. Her fingers snapped the box shut and tightened around it. She realized Kyra had started to speak, not knowing she was talking with Carter.

"Betha, it contains power from one of the archangels of the Heavens. You can't just give it back. I said I would give it to you, and now you have it. Keep it at least until I leave."

"Fine, I'll figure out what to do with it," muttered Betha. It made more sense now why Kyra had wanted to talk in person instead of over the phone. "So, I take it I am leaving in a few days?"

"That's up to you. To be honest, you need to be careful with volunteering to travel off Terra. You are so young." Kyra didn't meet her eyes.

"Kyra, I am twenty-one. I am an adult."

"Not to Travelers. We are long-lived. Usually, we stay with our parents or other family until we are a century or more. The traditional ceremony of adulthood is held on your one-hundredth birthday. That's when you are considered grown and allowed to leave home," answered Kyra.

"What?" Betha couldn't even imagine living to a hundred, let alone that she was considered not an adult until then. Everything she had dealt with in the last six months washed over her. From her mother's memory going, to heading to college, then all the portal and demon trouble. How could she not be considered an adult?

"You don't know anything about the Tree of Life or how portals work. It's dangerous out there," said Kyra softly.

"Children are dying—what more do I need to know?" asked Betha, exasperated.

Kyra's lips pressed together, and she closed her eyes for a moment. "Travelers are a wanted group in many of the worlds of the Tree. We used to be hunted down and captured. On Terra, there has been only me, and I've got a position of authority, so you are relatively safe. Though, I'm sure you remember that the whole council wanted—and still wants—to control you. We usually don't admit what we are to anyone, and we—"

"And how would I know that? It's not like you have been forthcoming with information," interrupted Betha. She was beginning to be truly angry and a little afraid. If she didn't know this, what else had Kyra never made time to mention?

"I thought we would have plenty of time now that the demons are gone! I don't want you to make any mistakes that trap you," replied Kyra.

"There is no way saving children from demons could possibly be a mistake. Even if it is, it is mine to make." Betha stood from the picnic table. "I know I will make mistakes. It's how you learn and grow as a person. That's something my mother taught me." Betha stormed away from the table with the wooden case in her hand.

Her anger flicked inside of her like a fire. Her fingers shook as she marched away, and everything churned. Betha clenched the wooden box in her fingers. She needed to breathe. The more she breathed, the more she realized this wasn't just *her* anger.

A figure jogged toward her and slowed down. At least this time he had a shirt on, though that first encounter seemed so long ago now. "You look like you have a bee in your bonnet," said Carter. The bond inside her stretched toward him. Some of this anger was his. Somehow she knew it was leaking through the bond. Betha had no idea how he was hiding this much rage.

"Do you think I did the wrong thing by offering to help Sir Samson?" demanded Betha.

Carter continued his jogging in place and his brow drew together. "I think it remains true to who you are as a person. If you can help someone, you will. It's one of the things that I appreciate about you." His words were soft. "Wait, who thinks it's a bad idea?"

Betha held up the box. "Kyra stopped by to give me the bounty from the prince, and the conversation devolved from there."

"Don't let her get to you. I can't imagine being stuck on Terra all these years. Plus, dealing with the council can't be fun." Carter motioned toward the box. "Also, don't lose that. The contents of that box were brought up at the council, and yeah, plenty of people want that."

"Really? I mean, what can it do?" Everyone kept making it sound like it was such a big deal.

Carter glanced around and shook his head. "How about we have this conversation somewhere else?"

"Sure, my dorm room is close by." Betha headed down the sidewalk toward the building she had been aiming for. They climbed the steps to the second floor and then it hit her that she was leading Carter back to her dorm room. Which was basically an extra-large bedroom with a bathroom attached.

"Is that your room?" asked Carter. He pointed to her door, which was slightly ajar.

"Well, fuck," Betha said, nodding.

He stepped in front of her and pulled a gun out from under his shirt. Betha's jaw dropped, wondering how he'd had that hidden so well. Tailored clothing for the win. He motioned her to stay behind him and nudged the door open. Then he vanished inside. A few seconds later, he swung the door open.

"Whoever they were, they are gone now," he said.

Betha entered the room and saw that all of her stuff was rifled through. Her bed was stripped, and every drawer emptied. The bathroom was even messed up, with the towels tossed on the floor.

Carter spoke to someone on his phone, then turned to her. Mentally he reached out. *"Is anything missing?"*

Betha shook her head and continued out loud. "Nothing seems to be gone. My bag is at Angie's since I was there last night."

He nodded and then responded on the phone to someone before hanging up. "Let's grab some of your stuff, and you can stay with Angie."

It didn't take long for her to pack up her clothes.

She really didn't have much. The single most impor-tant item was hidden in her right boot, and the feather was still in its box. Betha pulled the feather out and fit it into her boot with the knife. Her body armor was out of its bag, but it hadn't been touched.

"You like to travel light," joked Carter as he picked up her duffle bag.

Betha shrugged. "I mean, I don't really have a lot. I sold everything to get my mom into St. Luna's. And we never were big on stuff before that." He didn't respond, and Betha blushed. "I mean, I have the scrapbook and my boots. Which I didn't get to thank you for. They are absolutely perfect."

His response was interrupted as two Guards entered the room. They turned to Carter immediately. "Sir, we will get the place fingerprinted, and a wolf volunteered to try to sniff them out."

"Let me know if you find anything. We will get out of your way," said Carter.

Betha took that as the time to leave and headed out to the hallway.

"I'm glad you weren't here last night," said Carter. "It seems you can't catch a break."

Betha shrugged. These days, it seemed par for the course.

His eyes flickered down to her feet, and he smiled brightly. "I hoped you would like the boots. It seemed only right that a Traveler should have a great pair of boots for walking."

Betha couldn't help but laugh—she knew the song

he was referencing. "I guess this means I need to be more careful on campus... Again."

"Unfortunately. I know that you can handle yourself with a blade, but you don't carry one." In her head, he added. *"Given that we are leaving tonight, it doesn't really matter."*

"Tonight? I thought we had until tomorrow?" asked Betha in her head.

"It has something to do with traveling through the fey world. Day and night are shifted."

"Can we at least nap at Angie's?" Betha blushed as she realized what she had asked him.

"While a nap sounds fantastic, I need to pack my gear and probably a pack for you as well. Have you ever gone camping?"

Betha turned to look at him, her eyes wide. "Camping? No, I have never camped."

"This will be fun then!"

THE LAST TIME Betha had gathered around a doorway in the Nexus with her friends, things had not gone as planned. At least this time it wasn't a solo mission. She smiled at Carter and Angie, thankful to have at least some of her family with her.

There were a few others in the room, and she was doing her best to ignore one of them. She kept her gaze off of Kyra. While she knew that Kyra was her only source of Traveler information, what little Kyra had shared just angered Betha. At the moment, Traveler culture seemed very backwater, and she was glad her mother had raised her on Terra.

Joey had an arm around Angie, and Betha couldn't help but sneak a photo with her phone. Electronics wouldn't survive a portal crossing, so Eric nudged her with his elbow and she handed the phone off to him. *"Well, looks like she took your dating advice and things are still going well,"* she directed at him. Eric had given Angie dating advice several weeks ago, on the road trip to close one of the portals. Prior to his Anchoring, he'd been a bit of a player, and knew a lot about how to build relationships, even good ones.

A smirk flashed on his face, which then went blank. The sound of others entering the room caused Betha to look up. Sir Samson and Lord Seth came in with Grandpappy, whose shoulders were rather straight for some reason. He looked like someone had yanked on his tail.

"Ah, here is the rest of the party," commented Kyra.

Angie turned to Joey and kissed his lips softly before pulling back and whispering in his ear. All of the Anchors did their best not to listen in, but Joey's response wasn't whispered back. "Stay safe and come home. That's all I ask."

Grandpappy approached, and Joey stepped back, blushing ever so slightly. He patted Joey on the back and grinned at Angie. "You guys have this. Just don't stay out wandering the worlds too much," said Grandpappy. "I'd like to see you both again soon."

Betha replied, "Don't worry, we will help Sir Samson with his portal problem and be on our way back."

Grandpappy didn't look convinced, but he kept his

lips shut. It surprised Betha that he didn't voice his opinion. He always had in the past.

Lord Seth cleared his throat. "As touching as this is,
it's time to discuss particulars. Sir Samson will be traveling with you, along with one of his warriors. One of the
angels in the Fey realm will join you as well—they are
currently guarding the other side of the portal. May the
Heavens light your path."

Sir Samson stared at Betha and motioned for her to
go first. "Starwalker, will you lead the way?" asked the
gargoyle.

Betha's eyebrows drew together, but she nodded. It
seemed weird for her to lead since she had no idea how
to get where they were going. "Sure, off we go." With
that, she approached the portal. To her surprise Kyra
stood next to it. She stared at Betha and looked sad. It
was strange. Betha was missing something. Between
Grandpappy and now Kyra's look, was going such a bad
idea? Yet, she couldn't let doubt cloud her judgment. Her
path was set.

"Stay safe, Betha. Carter and Angie, make sure you
watch the troublemaker," commented Eric.

Betha stepped into the glowing light with a grin.
Since when was *she* the troublemaker?

ERIC WASN'T PREPARED for the bonds in the back of his
mind to be cut off. When Betha had gone through the
portal to the angelic realm, she had faded from the back
of his mind. But now his brother was gone too, and he

missed him. Everything with Betha had brought them together again, closer than they had been in years, and he didn't want it to end. The feeling of his brother in the back of his mind had brought him joy. Only a few months of that closeness, and he had gotten used to it.

Now it was silent.

At least he was going to be busy until everyone came back. Susan had texted him earlier, asking him to let her know once he was available. She had something she wanted to talk to him about. On top of that, he still needed to touch base with Kellion to find out what was going on with Lord Seth.

Hopefully, it wouldn't be long, and nothing would go to hell again while they were gone. They would be back. And this time, he was more prepared. He gave one last glance at the portal his new family had gone through, then he turned and headed out of the room. Right now, he needed to focus on what he could do to help—and distract—himself.

CHAPTER

SIX

The evening had somehow shifted. The bright light that greeted Betha on the other side of the portal was of high noon. The trees were a brilliant green that did not match the evergreen of where they were from on Terra. She lifted a hand, blocking some of the glaring brightness, but didn't stop moving forward. Blocking the doorway of the portal would not be a good idea.

Seconds later, Angie darted through the portal, almost running into her anyway. Betha grabbed her arm and jerked them both to the side.

"Ah, they have arrived," whispered an unknown voice. Angie spun around and placed Betha behind her. An angel and the gargoyle stood nearby under a tree.

"I think that's the guards," said Betha as the portal shimmered again. Sir Samson came through, followed quickly by Carter.

"Sir Samson!" said the other gargoyle as he appeared. This new gargoyle was smaller and seemed younger, with shorter black hair. The gargoyle moved forward, his arm outstretched. He had on a necklace that dangled down over his chest. It had a piece of polished wood with one end dipped in white paint. It was small but stood out against his dark skin color.

"Derrik, good to be by your side again," replied Sir Samson, taking the outstretched hand. Sir Samson turned to the rest of them with a grin. "We should cover ground before nightfall. The Fey Wilds can be tricky at the best of times, and night is not the best of times." He glanced up at the sky and nodded.

Carter smiled and held out a bag to Betha. "You forgot this," he said with a snicker. Angie shook her head as Betha went to grab the hiking bag.

"I totally left it behind," replied Betha, her face turning red. She picked the bag up and swung it over her shoulders, surprised at how light it was. "At least I have friends on this trip, watching my back."

"You are stuck with me like glue," responded Angie.

Somehow Betha hadn't noticed that Angie had a small backpack on as well. "How come yours is smaller?"

"If I need to change, I can keep it on. You and Carter have all the good stuff."

That made sense, and Betha felt a little dumb for asking. The bags made it clear that this wasn't going to be a walk in the park. Her cheeks deepened to a darker red when she realized that Sir Samson, Derrik, and the angel were watching their interaction with fascination. She turned toward Sir Samson. "Which way now?"

"This way." He motioned down a wide path into the trees. Derrik jumped up and spread his wings, taking to the clouds. "He will keep us on track. Normally we fly."

"Yeah, unless you can carry Angie, and that would be hard," said Betha jokingly.

"If needed, I can carry you, Starwalker," answered Sir Samson. Betha just looked at him, not sure how to respond. She hadn't considered actually flying and hoped it wouldn't be necessary.

"My name is Parian," said the angel into the awkward silence. He stepped forward. "I will join you on the ground for now." He wore armor and two swords strapped to his waist. He gave a nod to Carter. Despite being on foot, his wings were out.

Carter held out a hand. "I'm Carter. That's Betha and Angie."

"You must be Lord Seth's son. The resemblance is striking," answered Parian. "I heard you recently manifested. We need to make sure you get enough time flying to strengthen your wings." He paused as he saw an expression begin to darken Carter's face, then continued. "That came out wrong. I apologize. My son manifested right before I was called to serve in the Seventh Host. I keep slipping into training mode."

It was strange—Parian seemed so friendly for an angel. From what Betha knew, they were always stuck up jerks. Yet, Parian was offering to help Carter with what seemed to be no strings attached. He was making an effort to be on Carter's good side, and that wasn't what Betha had expected.

Sir Samson took the lead with Angie and Betha behind him. Carter and Parian took up the rear. They began chatting almost immediately about training, flying, and swords, and Betha turned her attention to their surroundings. The path was a dirt road, and the trees stopped two feet before the dirt started on either side. It was almost like home, but the green was off. She couldn't put a finger on it, but it wasn't like Terra. The color of the sky was strange as well, the blue too dark for the time of day and the amount of sunshine.

"I guess we don't need to worry about being quiet," whispered Betha.

"No, this area is relatively safe. Tomorrow, we need to be careful deeper in the woods," answered Sir Samson. "The fey keep an eye on the trade pathways. Trade is important to them. You probably won't see any, though. They don't like to disturb travelers on the trade paths."

Betha's shoulders relaxed at his words. It was easy to breathe here. The air wasn't heavy, and it was close enough to the air at home.

Angie pointed at some bright pink and blue flowers. "That isn't normal." The flowers were singing a soft melody, yet they didn't have mouths.

"Depends on your world," interjected Samson. "Each world is different. Singing flowers here means it is safe. Silent flowers mean danger."

It dawned on Betha that she knew nothing about the fey world or the desert world that they needed to cross. Her survival depended on her Anchors and the guards with them. The grudge she was holding against Kyra softened. The older Traveler's concern made sense—she really didn't know anything about the situation, and she had volunteered without learning anything. The sad look on Kyra's face came back to her, along with Grandpappy's reminding them to come home. It puzzled her. She grudgingly admitted that she didn't know what she was doing, but still, it seemed like she was in pretty good company. How bad could it be?

At least her boots were comfortable.

CARTER DIDN'T LIKE how Samson kept looking at Betha. There was something there that he didn't understand. Parian was happy to walk beside him, chatting about his son and the training program he had put together. He was so earnest and forthcoming with knowledge. It didn't match what Kellion had taught him growing up.

"So, is your son half like me?" asked Carter.

Parian nodded. "Not exactly like you, but close. His mother came over on a pilgrimage. More than half, but not much more. He is my first. I couldn't imagine having twins like you and your brother. Or having to leave my son behind. Lord Seth is the leader of the Eighth Host—he has responsibilities I would never want."

Carter bit his tongue from responding about his father. "What do you do when the angels aren't at war?"

Parian blinked. "I train new angels. Hence my comment about your wings. We really should take a turn in the sky and work on stretching. Your prowess in battle has preceded you but the sky is its own skill to master." He motioned to his own wings, which were out. "You should keep your wings out in case of trouble. Easy access to the sky."

"After the next water break, maybe we can head skyward." Carter didn't know how to respond about his wings. It had taken so long to get them to vanish after they appeared. Keeping them out hadn't even dawned on him.

"What does it mean to be anchored with the Traveler?" asked Parian. "I don't understand the stories. It isn't like my bond with my wife, is it?"

Carter blushed. "No, nothing like that. Angie and my brother are also anchored with Betha. We help one another and make each other stronger. It's complicated."

"It's like a host of angels then," stated Parian. "We strengthen one another. We are a host together and unstoppable. It is a tight bond."

He didn't know much of the hosts, only that they seemed like a team, but maybe it was more than that. It seemed he didn't know as much as he thought he did about the angels. Samson called for a water break near a stream that was close to the path. Carter approached Betha and Angie. "I am going to take a turn flying with Parian."

Angie nodded. "I'll shift for a bit since we will have fewer people on the ground." She turned her back to the group and stripped down without waiting for a response. Angie stuffed her clothes and shoes into her bag and loosened the straps. Then she was a giant black wolf. She nudged Betha, who was looking away.

"Can you fix my bag?" asked Angie.

Betha quickly adjusted the straps on the wolf until she nodded. Angie then started to sniff everything.

Betha gave Carter a smile as he also pulled off his bag. His armor had been modified to give him room for his wings. That was now a spot he had to be careful of since it was unarmored. Having an obvious weakness wasn't something he'd had to deal with before. Betha gasped as his wings shimmered into view. Her eyes traveled down each feather. Carter spread his wings out so she could get a better view. "A very different look, right?"

Betha blushed. "It is different, but it fits you. Your complexion is also different, like you have an inner light."

"He does," interrupted Parian. "Now that he manifested, he is filled with angel fire. It protects his soul."

"Does it?" Betha asked. She reached down to the bond she had with Carter. It had changed when she had forced his manifestation—bright light twisted around it. Yet Eric's bond wasn't like that, and she didn't know why.

"Yes, though now is the time to fly," said Parian.

Carter went to pick up his backpack, but Samson approached. "I'll take the bag. You should focus on flying." The gargoyle slid the bag on his front so it wouldn't affect his wings. "I'll give it back when Parian says you're ready. Parian is a good teacher."

"Thank you, Sir Samson. I do my best," answered Parian. He took off, jumping into the air.

Carter gave Samson a smile. "I appreciate it. Thank you." He quickly followed Parian skyward. Derrik watched them take off, gave them a thumbs up, and then headed toward the ground.

DERRIK LANDED SOFTLY on the dirt and gave Sir Samson a nod. With Parian in the air, it only made sense for him to land. With the other angel flying, Derrik realized that the remaining woman must be the Starwalker.

A giant wolf padded around the clearing, and he couldn't help but study it. The back of his neck itched—everything in him said to take to the skies and flee the giant black wolf.

"Derrik, she is with the Starwalker," whispered Sir Samson.

His shoulders relaxed at his words. It was hard ignoring his instincts to be in the air away from the wolf. They didn't walk often, but he could do this. All of his training had brought him here, and he would serve his people. The Starwalker was going to save them all. No matter what, she needed to get to Sky World, and he needed to be patient.

"Yes, Sir," he replied after settling himself.

Sir Samson had lost so much, and he was here, forced to walk as well. He could do this. The Starwalker smiled at him, and Derrik flashed his teeth in return.

"How was your flight?" asked the Starwalker.

Derrik blinked. How did one describe flying to someone who couldn't? Well, he spoke of it to the littles back home. He would try that.

"The sky was welcoming today," he whispered.

The wolf circled behind them, taking the rear guard, and he flinched.

"Angie won't hurt you," said the Starwalker. "She is making sure nothing sneaks up on us. She will vanish in a moment."

Derrik didn't understand all of the words. How would a wolf vanish? It didn't make sense. Yet, he turned back, and the wolf was gone. The Starwalker acted like this was normal. It must be. He could feel the power from the one beside him. The ones that walked with her must be powerful as well. This, he could understand.

He would watch and learn. The Starwalker acted like they were a clan. A strange clan filled with different types of people, but still a clan. The more he thought about it, the more it made sense. Starwalkers were from everywhere—they would bond with everyone.

It seemed he had more to learn, especially now. Learning could be a burden, but he would bear it. He would serve his people. The necklace he wore felt heavy, even though it was made of wood. It was the weight of his responsibility, and he knew the necklace was only the symbol. He would help save his people.

It seemed like they'd been walking forever, the angels and gargoyles taking turns flying and being on their feet with Betha. Derrik, flying high above them, wound downward in a circle before landing on the road. He spoke in an unknown language, though for some reason, Betha felt like she should know it. The more she heard it, the more it was like the words were just out of reach.

Sir Samson replied, then Derrik jumped back up and flew on ahead.

"There is a resting point soon," said Samson. Twenty

minutes later, the gargoyle led them off the road between two random trees. Betha couldn't tell them apart from any of the others. Yet, as they turned off the path a trail she hadn't noticed opened up into a small clearing. She tried not to show her relief as she slid the bag off of her shoulders.

Angie sniffed around the clearing. *"There is a stream over here where we can refill our water bottles. Can you get this bag off me so I can shift?"*

Betha quickly moved over to Angie, loosening the bag on the wolf's back. She averted her gaze as her friend regained her human form and pulled out her clothes from the bag.

"I haven't had a walk that long in my wolf form since this past summer," said Angie. "It felt good. Are we stopping here for the night?"

Sir Samson nodded. "Yes, the dark comes fast here. One moment it is daylight, the next there is no light." He pulled cut wood hidden behind a tree to the center of the clearing. "The fey keep the firewood supplied so no one tries to hurt the trees."

"I'll grab water," said Angie. She grabbed Betha's canteen, along with Carter's, before heading into the trees. Betha had no idea how to help. Everyone seemed to take a job from some unknown list.

"Betha, want to help me with the bedrolls?" asked Carter. She turned in his direction, relief in her eyes. He tossed a bedroll her way and motioned to put it near the fire. It didn't take long for her to figure out how to unroll it. She reached down again to the bond she had with Carter. He seemed less angry here, which was good. And the twisting light seemed more comfortable after he had taken a turn flying.

"Will Angie catch us a rabbit?" asked Parian.

"No," replied Betha before Angie could. "We have rations, and we don't know what kind of creatures are out there." Both gargoyles nodded, but the angel looked confused. Carter whispered something to him, and he shrugged.

"Don't you have a bedroll?" asked Betha to Sir Samson. He shook his head. "We sleep in the trees when we are not home." He motioned up at one of the towering trees above them. "We will keep watch."

Angie returned from the stream with a confused look on her face. "The fish taunted me and then tried to bite. I don't like this place."

Betha dug into her pack to see what she could find and pulled out a cooking pot, along with what looked to be a freeze-dried meal. "I think I found dinner. We might need some more water though." She held up the package.

Carter chimed in, "Yeah, that would make a good meal tonight. It will be quick over the fire." Angie grabbed the pot and headed back to the stream. This time she returned much quicker. Sir Samson got the fire started using two stones from his satchel. Then it was like someone turned off the lights. One moment, it was close to evening, then the light vanished, and it was dark.

"Whoa, that's amazing," whispered Angie.

Betha shivered. Usually, she liked the dark and the stars, but this darkness wasn't the same. Her eyes moved to the heavens as everyone in the group moved closer to the fire. No stars yet.

Carter took over cooking the stew and kept poking the fire.

"How long until we reach the next portal?" asked Betha.

Sir Samson glanced at the other gargoyle. "Hopefully tomorrow night. Flying only takes one day."

"Wasn't Garruk going to be joining us?" asked Betha.

Carter shook his head. "His group will be heading in this direction in a few days. It was going to take them longer to mobilize, and we wanted to get there as quickly as we could."

Sir Samson watched Carter as he spoke. "Yes, the green one will come later."

"Are you actually cousins?" asked Betha.

Sir Samson's eyes narrowed, and he looked toward the angel. "Cousins?" he repeated.

"Gargoyles and trolls, I mean," clarified Betha.

Parian responded in a different language, and Samson replied back. The language was just there, just out of reach. She felt like she should be able to understand it.

To her surprise, it was Parian who responded. "Trolls and gargoyles are distantly related, many thousands of years in the past. The gargoyles were surprised to see the trolls on Terra since they thought all had fallen to the demons."

Angie jumped in this time. "Fallen to the demons? How long has this been going on?"

Parian sat back on his own bedroll with a smile. "I

guess I will start at the beginning." He rubbed his hands together near the fire.

"Demons only had one world, like all the rest of the races, but they were greedy. They pushed into other worlds. Again and again, until they tried to take the Heavens. We pushed them back for the first time and swore not to let them take any other. They have six worlds as we speak—they call them circles. But they will not get a seventh! Sky World will not fall!"

"Holy smokes." Betha's mind went blank, staggering as too many thoughts were going at once. "We pushed them back from Terra."

"You are only the second world to do so," added Parian.

This wasn't the first time the demons had done this, and it wouldn't be the last. Betha's chest tightened, and her fists curled up.

An arm swung over her shoulder, and Angie patted her on the back. *"Breathe, we aren't going to solve the demon problem this week. We only need to help the gargoyles."*

Betha nodded and took a deep breath. She would help the gargoyles. One thing at a time. They would help Sky World and its children. Then, they'd deal with whatever was next.

ANGIE RESISTED TOSSING AND TURNING, but it was harder in her wolf form. Different scents came across the clearing on the breeze, and she couldn't understand all of them.

This fey world was weird. Biting fish who talked back were just wrong. She knew fey had to be in the forest watching them, but she couldn't catch a glimpse. It was only her nose that let her know it wasn't as empty as it appeared.

It seemed they did not have all of the information about the demons or gargoyles. She couldn't help but catch the looks and feelings coming from Betha. Her best friend had too big of a heart sometimes. This trip was to save the gargoyles, and the next one would be to save someone else. It was why Angie stuck so close. Betha would give and give until she didn't have anything left. Angie had to make sure Betha didn't give until she wasn't there anymore.

It had happened with her mom. Betha had taken care of her, worked thirty hours a week at a coffee shop and then taken classes full-time at night. Thankfully, the fates had intervened, and the acceptance to St. Luna's had come through, along with that financial assistance. Betha had been at her breaking point, with dark bags under her eyes, way too skinny from skipping meals and bills stacked on the counter. Not to mention the amount of caffeine she was drinking. It had worried Angie and Grandpappy both.

Thankfully, Betha had pulled herself together and made the opportunity presented work. Now, Angie was worried about it happening again. This journey to help the gargoyles, learning about what the demons were doing—it all worried her. But she knew what she was doing was right and this was a hill Betha was willing to die on.

Angie got up and padded across the campsite close to Betha. She curled up next to her friend in her bedroll. Sleeping in her wolf form was more comfortable than lying on one of those blankets, and being closer to Betha felt right. It calmed the anxiety in her wolf. They would figure this out. They would help the gargoyles and then go home. Angie would make sure of it.

She remembered the glance Grandpappy had sent her way after Betha had gone through that portal. Her job was to get Betha back to Terra after this. She didn't know how she would do it, but she knew she would try.

A PARTIAL MOON shone down on her, and Betha couldn't help but smile. This recurring dream—or whatever it was—always felt safe. She hadn't been sure if she could visit this place while not on Terra, and she hadn't known what she would do without it. That worry was now washed away as peace came over her. Fireflies drifted around her in a light breeze that caressed the comfortable grass under her.

Her right foot was warm, and it took her a moment to realize that it was the knife. Betha carefully removed it from the hidden sheath and almost dropped it out of surprise. It glowed like the fireflies. The tattoo on her wrist sparkled in response, pulsing to the same pattern as the fireflies and the knife.

"I don't know who died to create you, but you are safe now. I won't let anyone else use you to cause harm." Her voice was soft in the night. Being here was like a warm, comforting hug from her mom. The feeling of rightness washed over her, and Betha smiled.

"We will save the gargoyles and stop the demons. We did it once, and we can do it again."

Betha leaned back and set the knife beside her in the grass. It would be all right. She just knew it.

CHAPTER

SEVEN

The campsite was quiet as dawn broke over the tall trees. Betha had fallen asleep after staring at the stars. They were not the stars she knew from Terra, but still, they had let her relax enough to stop twitching at every sound. The smell of coffee wafted over, seeming out of place, but she wasn't going to resist it.

Angie sat near the edge of the fire, quickly pouring the drink into a thermos. *"I got some coffee here for you, just give it a moment to cool."*

Betha couldn't help but smile as she quickly rolled up the sleeping bag she had been using.

"You brought coffee!"

Carter wandered over toward Angie. "You brought instant coffee?"

Angie smirked and motioned toward Betha. "It's not for me. Betha gets weird without coffee. She needs a cup a day to keep the healer away."

Betha blushed as she pulled on the armor she had taken off last night. Everyone was moving at their own pace, but it seemed they would be leaving shortly. Sliding on the boots was a wonderful experience. She still wished she knew what magic was in them. The best part was her feet did not hurt at all, and she knew they should with all of the walking yesterday.

"Your elixir, my dear," said Carter.

She snapped her eyes up as he squatted down next to her holding out the thermos. Angie wasn't at the fire anymore, but Betha could feel her over where the stream was.

"Thank you. Angie's right—coffee is one of my weaknesses."

"I don't know how I didn't know that," said Carter.

"Well, I used to work at a coffee shop before I came to St. Luna's. My goal was to eventually open up my own place or take over where I used to work after university. Now, I just like some caffeine in the morning." Betha felt like she was rambling, but she couldn't get over the fact he called her "my dear." She wasn't sure if it was him joking. It rattled her, but in a good way.

"I will have to keep that in mind and pack some on our next trip."

Her boots were on, and it was time to stand up, yet she didn't move. He was right there with a perfect smile and his blue eyes seemed to sparkle. Carter stood, breaking the moment, and offered her a hand. He helped her pull herself up from the ground and then they were really close. Betha stared into his eyes, then he held out the coffee again. This time she took it, taking a step back. The butterflies in her stomach would need to wait.

"The boots do look good on you," he said softly.

"Time to move!" called out Sir Samson.

Carter's lips snapped shut, and he gave a nod to Betha. "Guess it's time we grab our bags and set off again."

"Yep, time to get back to work," said Betha. She frowned at the backpack at her feet. Picking it up again was going to be hard.

Angie headed her way with a goofy grin. *"You know you can just act normal around him, right?"*

Betha swung the bag onto her shoulders and realized it was lighter than it had been the day before. Using food out of it last night had helped.

"I know, I just freeze. And my thoughts get tangled. I wanted to kiss him for the coffee," answered Betha.

Angie slung an arm around her waist and pulled her into a small hug. *"It will all work out. Just have faith."*

The group quickly took up the same formation they had the day before. Derrik took to the skies, and Carter with Parian took up the rear. Sir Samson took the lead but motioned Betha up with him. He looked away as Angie stripped and then shifted. The giant wolf nudged Betha to fix her bag before moving to walk in front of the gargoyle.

"Tonight, we go to the next portal," stated Sir Samson. "Then it's the hot sand, but only for a short time. Then to Sky World." He grinned, showing bright white teeth, some of which looked pointed.

"Good, I don't mind the hiking, but I am excited to see your world," answered Betha.

Sir Samson's brows moved closer together, and his eyes softened. "It's not what it was. Once the demons are gone, you can stay and learn from our elders. Starwalkers are important, especially to us."

"Why do you call me a Starwalker?" asked Betha.

He looked confused. "You walk among the stars. Old gargoyle stories. We know what you are. The elders will tell more in Sky World."

Betha nodded, but she was confused. It sounded like the older gargoyles knew about Travelers, and they wanted to teach her. Yet, Kyra did not react well to the name Starwalker. The more she heard, the more answers she wanted. They expected her to stay after she helped them with the demons. She wasn't so sure about that. Mentally, she shook her head. She just didn't know enough to make that decision, and she knew there wasn't a point in worrying about it right now.

Carter took up the rear guard with Parian, who was a treasure trove of information. It was a world of a difference from working with Eric. While Carter loved his brother, learning from him was difficult, especially surrounding anything related to being an angel.

Betha's voice washed over him, and he wished he knew what she was talking about with Samson. He couldn't help the small smile that came to his lips as she laughed.

The morning passed quickly, and the sun rose tall in the sky.

"Do you think we should stop soon for lunch?" asked Carter.

Parian shook his head. "I think I know where we are stopping. We have around another hour, but there is a nice stream to take a break. It was a great stopping point when we came this way for the council meeting. Of course, we were flying, so I might be off."

Carter chuckled. "I can imagine that translating flying speed to walking speed is not something you do much of."

"You get used to it," answered Parian. "This afternoon I'll show you how I figure it out, when I have to."

Betha slowed her pace and turned toward them. Once they caught up, she fell in line between the two of them. "Hey, I guess there is a swimming hole at the next break."

"I, for one, will not be swimming in this world," answered Parian. "I don't like to get wet."

Betha laughed, and Carter almost stumbled. He could feel her joy through the bond, and it was so refreshing. It was better than the plans about keeping everyone—especially Betha—safe going through his head. The unknowns of Sky World, plus the demonic forces they'd be facing, kept his joy in check.

"Didn't Angie mention biting fish?" asked Carter.

Betha shrugged in response. "I doubt I am going to go swimming, but I might be tempted. You never know."

"See, that's only because you haven't gone flying," added Parian. "Flying is a wonder like no other. Much better than swimming."

"I bet. Someday I hope to experience it."

"I can take you up this afternoon, if you like," responded Parian.

Carter couldn't help himself, and he glared at Parian over Betha's head. The older angel winked at him.

Betha took a moment to respond. "Maybe on the way back. I am going to catch up to Angie and Sir Samson."

To Carter, it seemed Betha was fleeing back toward the front of the group.

Parian moved closer to him. "She likes you. You know that right?"

Carter nodded automatically, and his thoughts froze. He wasn't sure how to respond. Betha had almost made a move several weeks ago, but then everything with her mother had happened. They needed to have a conversation, but the timing never seemed to work out. His eyes drifted down to her backside before he quickly clears his throat and looks elsewhere to try to focus on the challenges ahead. "I was drawn to her even before we anchored."

"Young love. Enjoy it while it lasts. Next thing you know, you are married and have little kids," sighed Parian. "Not that being married isn't amazing. It is."

Carter sighed in turn. "It's complicated. She's young."

Parian shrugged. "It doesn't need to be. Think about it while flying—that will set you straight. I mean, age hardly matters anymore. Not when war happens."

Carter had no idea how to respond to that. He had trained his whole life to become a Guard, but the honest truth was no one had expected to have to fight. Peace had reigned on Terra with the signing of the Accords. Small conflicts broke out, like a really old creature losing it after a millennium. That vampire had to be put down, but the daywalkers had done the deed rather than the Guard. And those types of things were taken care of quickly and quietly.

This was different. He liked Betha, and he cared for her. His eyes focused on her back and her brown hair. She saw him for him and never cared that he was human. Not that he was human anymore. But neither was she.

BETHA COULD FEEL Carter's eyes on her, and she couldn't help but wonder what it meant. The urge to see if she could hear what he and Parian were talking about was hard to resist.

Instead, she focused on the bright sunny day and that Sir Samson said that they were close to stopping for lunch. This world was so different from Terra. The colors were much more intense. The greens and blues of the tree leaves and the bright flowers were almost glowing. It was weird that they hadn't heard any animals or birds though. She remembered that Sir Samson had said they probably wouldn't see any fey, but she found that strange too. She didn't know how it all made her feel. Part of her hoped she would see the fish that wanted to bite Angie in the stream up ahead. At least that would be something more than the endless trees.

"Ah, we are almost there," said Sir Samson. The gargoyle in the sky came closer in a downward spiral until he vanished over some trees. "Derrik landed. Come."

Angie's dark form took off down the trail, racing ahead. *"Last one there is a slow poke!"*

Carter chuckled in response.

Betha couldn't resist the challenge and picked up her pace, racing down the trail. Laughter flowed out of her, and she enjoyed how much faster she had gotten. It was such a difference from before she had been anchored. Running was just so much easier.

The trees thinned out into a clearing, and a bridge over a large creek appeared. Angie flopped to the grass, panting. Derrik stood by the bridge, keeping an eye further down the trail. The sunlight streamed down, and logs formed a modest fire pit. This was clearly a regular stop for anyone traveling the path.

"Ah, see. Worth waiting," said Sir Samson.

Betha walked closer to Angie. *"Well, at least I am not the slow poke."* She dropped her bag and let it softly hit the ground. Her shoulders ached, and she started to stretch them out. She turned back toward the trail they had come from and watched Carter and Parian slowly come into view.

"Carter is the slow poke," joked Angie. *"Running felt good. I miss running in the mountains."*

Betha sat down on the grass next to her friend and leaned against her giant form. *"Maybe after this we can spend a few weeks up there. We could invite Joey and have a few weeks of camping. It could be fun."*

It took a minute for Angie to respond. *"A few weeks is a long time to spend in the woods. You can tell you haven't gone camping before. Not to mention, I am not sure we would be welcome—the mountains are Pack lands. You aren't Pack, and I am anchored. But there are other places to go."*

Betha realized that Angie had a few walls up when her response came out flat. There wasn't any emotion attached to it. *"I bet you would be welcome no matter what. And I don't have to come. I can annoy Carter and Eric for a week. It will be fun. You don't need to be at my side all of the time. Grandpappy isn't always with Kyra."*

She reached out and petted Angie's side. If you took the fact that they were in a different world out of the picture, this could have been a moment from summers in their back yards. Of course, they weren't talking in each other's heads back then, either. The bond made it so much easier to have good conversations.

"Kyra doesn't go anywhere. She stays mostly at the Nexus. I would go crazy being constrained like that."

Betha snorted. *"You and me both."*

"Are you two going to be lazy? Or are you going to grab some food and join us?" asked Carter.

Betha glanced up and realized Parian, Sir Samson, and Derrik had gathered on some logs in the circle. "We're coming!" She slowly climbed to her feet, then Angie followed suit.

"I am going to sniff on up ahead. Keep me in the loop," said Angie before she trotted off toward the bridge.

Betha chuckled and headed toward the group of guys, wondering why it was so quiet near the group. "She is going to keep watch." Her eyes landed on Carter. His wings were out, and she softly smiled. They just fit him so well. Not that he wasn't amazing as a human, it was just that it seemed he was now, somehow, complete.

His eyes found hers, and Betha could feel the heat rushing to her cheeks. She looked away first. Thoughts of him jogging around campus shirtless came to mind. Her eyes landed on the bushes near the edge of the trees. Bright red eyes stared back.

Another set appeared, and another. Her chest felt tight and it was hard to breathe. That was the missing sound—the flowers had gone silent.

"In the bushes," she sent out on the bond, holding perfectly still. Carter jumped into action, spinning around, and then there was movement everywhere. A group of scaled, bright red monkeys darted out into the open. Long claws grew from each paw, and their tails had spikes on the ends.

Betha struggled to pull out her sword, but given Sir Samson, Parian, and Carter all attacked first, she had time. *Deep breaths, you got this.* Inside her head, she could feel Angie moving closer. They must have been clever to have approached so that Angie hadn't sensed them.

One of the creatures slipped by the group and headed right toward her. She dodged the swipe of the claws but wasn't prepared for a jab with its tail. It grazed her hand, but the cut wasn't deep. The pain unfroze her brain, and she could breathe again.

Cries came from the trees, and suddenly the creatures that were still standing all took off. A few red bodies were on the ground, but most of them fled. Betha's heart pounded as she turned, looking in each direction. Angie slowly made her way closer, her maw covered in blood.

"What were those?" asked Angie.

Carter moved closer to them. "I don't have any idea what those were."

"Half-breed demons called Piccum," spat out Parian. "They bred with wild fey. Normally, fey would have nothing to do with demonkind, since their lord would prevent it. Wild fey don't owe fealty to the fey lord, who is the ruler of the land. We haven't seen them around this area before, and they shouldn't be here. They usually keep to themselves."

Sweat broke out on Betha's forehead, and it was hard to breathe again. It was weird.

"*Betha?*" asked Angie, who was suddenly standing next to her. "*She doesn't smell right.*"

"I am okay," whispered Betha weakly.

"Did she get cut?" asked Parian.

Betha held up the back of her hand. A shallow cut crossed it. Heat pulsed from the wound. She could hear something being spoken, but it was in a language she didn't understand. The rhythm was familiar, though. Sir Samson's voice was rough.

Parian replied quickly, "We need to move. Their tails have poison on them, usually to slow down their targets before they eat them."

"She heals faster than a human," commented Carter. He moved closer to her, examining the wound. "The wound is trying to close."

Loud cries sounded in the trees, and the party froze.

"We must fly. I'll carry Angie. Betha goes with Parian," said Sir Samson. "We need distance between the half-breeds. Derrik, carry the packs."

Carter stepped away from Betha and grabbed the

bags. He quickly tossed clothing out into the clearing for Angie. Angie gave Betha a worried smile and grabbed some clothing. Betha couldn't believe that she hadn't realized her best friend had shifted.

Derrik grabbed the bags from Carter and consolidated them. Parian moved closer to Betha. "It looks like you are going to get that flight after all." His bright white wings spread out. "I will scoop up under your legs and back. Hold onto my neck lightly. Carter, pace yourself."

Parian moved forward, and Betha wrapped her arms around his neck. Her gaze landed on Carter. His eyebrows were drawn close together, and he was speaking to Derrik. The gargoyle motioned to the air, and Carter nodded. He caught her looking at him and flashed her a small smile.

"It will be okay," he whispered in her mind. *"Hold on."*

Parian scooped her up and then jumped into the air. Betha automatically closed her eyes. The air cooled down as they gained height. Screeches from down below caused her to tighten her arms around Parian's neck.

"Don't worry, they can't reach us now," replied Parian. "You can look—I won't drop you. You are lighter than my wife, and she loves to fly."

Betha focused on his words and opened her eyes. They were way above the trees, and she could see Sir Samson ahead of them, holding onto Angie. The cold air reduced the amount of sweat that had been forming on her brow. It felt refreshing at the moment, but part of her worried about how cold she was going to get.

"This isn't bad," whispered Betha. The sky was clear, and the trees passing by below didn't seem too far away.

Watching Sir Samson's shadow travel across the treetops was pretty cool.

"Maybe for you! This is horrible! My feet should never leave the ground ever again," Angie's voice trembled in her head.

"Deep breaths, Angie," replied Carter. *"Samson isn't going to drop you. The only reason we didn't do this sooner was because of me. I can't fly nonstop. They said the portal to the desert world is only an hour or so by flying."* Betha ignored the fact that Angie had gotten really bad motion sickness in the helicopter back on Terra. Hopefully, Sir Samson didn't get thrown up on. That wouldn't be very nice.

"I'll survive," answered Angie. *"How are you doing, Betha?"*

"My head hurts, and I am hot all over. I think I'm okay other than that." Suddenly, Betha realized something about what Parien had said earlier. Out loud, she asked Parian. "Your wife doesn't have wings?"

"No, she's human, from your world. We fell madly in love, and she moved to the heavens to be with me. I couldn't live without her. We have the most beautiful son."

It sounded so romantic, but at the same time, Betha was confused. She hadn't heard that humans could go to the heavens. Or that angels found wives on Terra. None of this made sense. Traveling to the heavens had almost killed her, or it felt like it at least. She thought the angels came to Terra to have sex and then they left the kids behind. That's what seemed to have happened to Carter.

"Is your son a Nephilim?" asked Betha.

"He manifested before I left. I hope he doesn't grow up too fast until I am back," answered Parian. "His wings are so adorable." Parien adjusted his grip on Betha. "Hmm, you are getting warm, Traveler."

Betha's hand began to hurt. It had hurt before, but it had just been a scratch—it hadn't been a big deal. Now, it *hurt*. Pain radiated down each of her fingers, and she couldn't move any of them. She could still feel her wrist, but her hand was locked around the back of Parian's neck.

What was worse was the pain moved quickly down her wrist into her arm. Then she couldn't feel her fingers anymore. Panic welled up, but she forced herself to take deep breaths. They were flying through the air, and there wasn't any more anyone could do. This was not the time to completely panic. Even if she wanted to.

EIGHT

Carter could feel the wall that Betha had erected in her mind slowly crumble. He wasn't sure if it was the poison or something else, but her emotions slipped slowly into the bond. His wings carried him through the air, and this was the fastest he'd ever gone. Derrik flew next to him carrying his backpack, along with Betha's. Carter's only job was to make it to the portal.

He hadn't trained enough for this. Fear crept along his spine, and he tried to focus on Sir Samson in front of him carrying Angie and Parian carrying Betha. Yet, that wall inside the bond was falling apart, and it made it hard to concentrate. The pain from Betha's hand was diluted, but the panic it was causing her wasn't.

Each flap of his wings was getting harder, and he could see that he was slowing down. Derrik kept pace with him and let the others pull on ahead.

"Betha, keep taking deep breaths. Sir Samson says we aren't far. We are making good time." Angie's voice was soothing, and it seemed to help Betha from what Carter

could sense. Her panic reduced slightly, and it let Carter regain his focus. He sped back up and was thankful for Angie's intervention.

"You got this, Betha," he added. *"We are right here with you."* He had no idea how far away the portal to the next world was. Only that they would make it, and that Betha would be okay.

"I can't feel my fingers," replied Betha.

"The poison is trying to paralyze you. Your healing abilities are fighting against it," said Carter.

"It's still spreading."

Her voice hit the pit of his stomach with a bang. Realization dawned on Carter that he wished he could wrap his arms around her and hold her close. That wasn't what he should be feeling for her, but it still ran through his heart.

"Carter!"

Carter glanced around frantically at Derrik's shout. He had gotten lost in his thoughts and had drifted lower in the sky. His eyes landed on the ground and the treetops. They were too close. In the distance, he could see creatures walking down the trail, but as they noticed them in the sky, they scattered.

"Up! Up!" The gargoyle darted in front of him, trying to get him to fly higher.

Carter aimed himself upward and beat his wings faster. His shoulders were getting tired, and his back muscles were straining. The flying he had been doing over the past week was not at such a fast pace.

He slowly regained altitude, wishing that he had spent more time in the sky. Parian had teased him about not worked enough on his wings, and now he felt it. It seemed he had not yet learned how to fly automatically either. This was something he needed to remedy. He had been treating his wings like something he could ignore instead of like a new part of him he needed to learn how to use. He swore to himself that would stop after this.

THE AIR SEEMED to get colder, and the numb feeling spread to Betha's elbow. She was thankful her arm was already around Parian. At this point, she wasn't sure if she could move it.

"We are so close, young Traveler. See that clearing up ahead?" asked Parian. Betha turned her head away from his neck and glanced forward. Sir Samson and Angie were flying lower in the sky, and it seemed they were aiming for a clearing. The clearing wasn't very large, but Betha realized she could sense something there—they were close to the portal.

It gave her hope. The journey was supposed to be the hike to the desert portal, then a quick hike across the hot sand to the portal to Sky World. They were close.

They descended toward the clearing, and fear gripped Betha again. She wasn't sure how the landing would go, and her body froze in panic.

"Don't worry, this will be easy. I am simply going to jump down," said Parian.

Betha closed her eyes and burrowed her face into his neck. The arm that she could control wrapped a little tighter around him. He chuckled in response.

"You can open your eyes now."

Betha's eyes snapped open, and he carefully set her on her feet. Immediately the portal stood out.

"He needs to be careful!" growled Parian. He wasn't looking in her direction at all.

Her eyes whipped around from looking at the opening to the sky. She could make out Derrik flying around Carter. She wasn't sure what he was saying, but it was clear Carter was struggling.

"Shit, I hope this wasn't too much for him." Angie's words almost caused her to jump, and her friend wrapped an arm around her waist. Angie twisted her hand to look at the wound. "It still looks the same," she commented. She leaned down and sniffed at it. "But it smells wrong."

The dot that was Carter came closer, and a sudden gust of air hit Betha. Parian darted into the sky, heading straight for Carter. He shouted something, and Carter stopped flapping his wings. Derrik then headed downward, landing in the clearing gracefully.

Finally, Carter glided toward the clearing and landed awkwardly on his feet.

"You need to let your wings rest. If you can vanish them, you should." Parian's tone was that of a patient instructor. The growling attitude had vanished.

"Well, we are all here. Betha, how is your hand?" asked Carter. His face looked strained, and his blond hair was all over the place.

"Numb," she replied. "Are you okay?"

Carter shrugged and winced. His wings vanished from view as his eyes grew wide. "That hurts!"

"It will until they rest. We pushed you too hard," said the older angel.

Sir Samson's voice stopped the conversation. "We must move if we don't want to deal with the sun in the desert."

Betha turned toward the gargoyle leader and realized he was right next to the portal. To her surprise, it was outlined by two trees right on the edge of the clearing. The branches wove around each other above it, creating a gateway. The air near the portal glimmered slightly, but that was it. The more she focused on it, the more she could taste dust—and maybe burned marshmallows. It was fascinating. She was unsure if she would ever look at marshmallows the same again.

"The night is ending on the sand," Sir Samson continued. "We must go now or wait."

"Let's go," answered Angie. "I don't think we should wait around here. We need to get Betha something for that poison. I'll shift if it's dark there."

Betha nodded. It made sense. "Yeah, I don't know how long I can walk."

"Don't worry, we will get you there," answered Carter.

Angie quickly stripped off the t-shirt and shorts she had tossed on before the flight. After the crunch of bones, her giant black wolf stood in the clearing. Carter helped her fix her bag, and he grabbed his own bag from Derrik.

Sir Samson took the bag that Betha had been carrying and motioned her forward. "I will go first, then you come through."

He vanished into the space between the trees and then Betha followed, cradling her arm.

TIME SEEMED to stop for a moment, and Betha could feel her mark itching. She swore she was in the in-between place with darkness and stars. Something she couldn't see touched her numb hand and arm. The in-between was the only place she had felt that warm touch.

"It's okay—my friends are helping me," whispered Betha to the faint presence.

Then heat hit her face and she was walking on rocky ground.

"*Betha!*" Angie's voice rang in her head, and the wolf brushed up against her hip.

"Thank the goddesses! You weren't here!" Carter's hand landed on her shoulder, and his bright blue eyes stared at her. "What happened?"

Everyone was staring at her, and she realized it was dark, but a sliver of a moon glowed overhead. The air was stuffy and hot, which was strange given how dark it was.

"I don't really know. I think I paused in-between."

"*Like before?*" asked Angie.

"She Starwalked," cut in Sir Samson. His eyes drew close together as he glanced between Angie and Carter. There was confusion on his face. "She is here now. Day is coming with the burning hot sun. We must go."

The moon was overhead, but light peeked over the horizon in the distance. Given how hot it already was, as evidenced by the sweat forming under Betha's armor, she did not want to feel how hot it would get in full daylight.

"I'm fine. Let's just get to Sky World," answered Betha. Angie nodded her snout and moved up close to Sir Samson. Betha could barely see her, even in the moonlight.

Carter let his hand fall away slowly. "We were worried. Angie and I appeared, and you weren't here."

"He was really worried," sent Angie. *"It was cute. I knew you would show up."*

"It's okay. I think the in-between was worried about my arm," said Betha.

"The in-between was worried about your arm?" asked Angie loudly.

Carter flinched as Angie spoke, so Betha assumed Angie was projecting to them both. Usually, Angie had the most control of any of them, but she was clearly more shaken than she was letting on.

"Yeah, it was just for a second, but it felt worried about my arm. I said you guys were helping to fix it. Then I was here." Betha shrugged. Her Anchors knew about the in-between and how she swore it was conscious like a person.

Walking across the sand was slow going, and everyone stayed quiet. Some sort of insects were making sounds like crickets back home, but it was super soft. That burnt marshmallow smell was gone, and instead, a clean earthy smell rose with each step across the sand. She wondered where the marshmallow smell had come from.

"Why aren't we flying?" Betha asked.

Carter shook his head. *"Samson said no flying in the dark. If it was the day we could, but not at nighttime."*

"Yeah, I see some things moving in the sky if I stare at it. I don't want to know what's up there," answered Angie.

Betha moved a little closer to Carter, who was walking beside her. Derrik and Parian were the rear guard.

"How is your arm?" asked Carter.

His question had been so loud in the darkness that it almost caused her to stumble. Carter reached out to grab her. His hand felt warm on her waist.

"The pain is gone, but the numbness is still there." She poked at her bicep and realized she couldn't feel it. "Yeah, my bicep is numb as well, but I can still rotate my shoulder."

Sir Samson paused, and Angie jerked to a halt.

"Don't move," said Angie. Sweetness filled the air— the crispy marshmallow smell was back.

Betha froze.

"What the fuck is that?" asked Angie.

She had no idea what her friend was seeing, but she could barely hear something sliding against the sand. Fear trickled down the bond, and Betha forced herself to repair the wall she usually kept up. She had no idea when it had fallen, but it was clear it was gone. Feeling all of her Anchors' emotions wouldn't help her here.

"It's moving away." said Angie.

Sir Samson stayed still for several minutes longer before he started walking again. The sweet smell took time to fade.

"I don't like this place," added Angie. *"Let's finish this job and find a different way home."*

Betha reached out with her senses and felt the portal they had left behind. To her surprise, she could also feel another portal ahead. It was much closer than she had expected. Giant dark rocks came into view as the light creeping over the horizon grew brighter. More came into view as the light rapidly increased. The temperature increased as well, and the whole party moved faster.

As they moved closer to the rock outcropping, Betha realized that there was an archway created by the rock. It didn't look like someone had made it, unless they'd sculpted it from flowing rock. It flowed from the ground up, then curved over. Not quite a perfect arch. It was jagged on one end, but it did create an opening. The air within the opening sparkled like liquid with flecks of gold glitter. The liquid was so white it was nearly blue as they approached. At the top, eyes seemed to peek out from the ridge, but they could have been imperfections in the stone.

Her shoulders relaxed as they walked closer and Sir Samson motioned Derrik forward. The younger gargoyle gave them a smile and then darted through the portal. He returned a moment later, said something in his language, then dashed back through. The sound of his voice, brief though it had been, seemed loud in the moments before true dawn.

Sir Samson motioned everyone to quickly get through the portal. Angie gave a nod to Betha and then jumped through. Parian was next, his blond hair flowing behind him. Sir Samson's waving them forward grew frantic. "Move!" The sound of something sliding over the sand reached her ears, and the smell of marshmallows filled her nose.

Carter glanced over his shoulder, but before Betha could look, he grabbed her hand and yanked her forward. They stumbled through the portal together and landed roughly on the other side. Sir Samson quickly came through, tripping over them on the ground.

A deep laughter broke out from Sir Samson as he climbed to his feet. "The great snake was so close!" His laughter sounded like it was from fear and uncertainty.

Derrik's face turned to one of panic, and Parian went pale.

"The sandworm came back?" Parian's voice was high-pitched, and he leaned against a tall tree. Sir Samson held out a hand and helped Betha to her feet. Now that she was off of Carter, he got up from the ground. She took a breath and looked around. The sky was a bright blue, and fluffy white clouds floated in the air. The trees were closer to what she was used to. She could swear that they were in a pine forest back on Terra.

The portal behind them was on a rock face that rose taller than she could see. Again, there was a natural divot in the rock that had glittery gold inside. This time, it wasn't an archway—more like an impression in the stone face. Something rested at the top, but she didn't get a good look.

Carter froze beside her but then relaxed. Betha realized that more people had gathered around the portal.

"Uncle!" called out a young voice.

A small, winged Gargoyle dashed out of the trees,

heading straight to Sir Samson. The lead gargoyle flashed his bright white teeth in that direction and picked up the little one, tossing him in the air. The young gargoyle's wings flapped rapidly, and he stayed afloat for but a moment before he came back down into Sir Samson's arms.

"Jadon, you are sneaky! You are supposed to be at camp, not here. The portal isn't safe for small bats."

"Oh Uncle, you came home!" The little one burrowed into his uncle's neck.

Betha couldn't help the grin that came to her face. More gargoyles came out of the shadows, several with spears and bows. They glanced around from tree to tree, clearly on edge. She held her arm tighter to her side and stepped closer to Carter. Angie stood over near the rocks, still in her wolf form.

"Leader Samson," chimed one of the winged fellows. "We need to move. This area isn't safe. The camp up above is safer. The elders are here."

Sir Samson's eyebrows drew together, and he bared his teeth. "The elders shouldn't be at Rock Camp. They should be at Mountain Hold."

The fellow glanced over his shoulder, then leaned in toward Sir Samson. "The demons have attacked several camps. The elders have fallen back to this location to wait for the Starwalker."

"*Man, they are being intense,*" said Angie, who had hidden in the shadows near the rock ledge. "*I wonder what they are saying.*"

"*What do you mean? He just said the demons attacked several camps,*" answered Betha.

"Uh, he just spoke in whatever language they speak, Betha."

"We need a healer." said Sir Samson. His gaze went toward the sky, but he froze as another voice called out.

"What happened to the Starwalker? Samson, shame on you!" called out a female gargoyle. She scurried to Betha's side. Surprisingly, she was around Betha's height and had blue tattoos on her face and wings. Most of the gargoyles she had seen so far had been taller than her. She wore leather pants and a simple band around her breasts. She motioned to Betha's damaged hand, and Betha showed it to the newcomer. The pain had started making her wobble.

"The Piccum demons got her," answered Sir Samson.

The short gargoyle female tsked. "Dumb leaders not taking care of guests." She quickly rummaged around in a hip bag and pulled out several leaves. She held them out, motioning for Betha to eat them. "I am Nalli. These leaves help with numbness. Since you are still upright, it hasn't traveled far in your body. Though you are burning up. Hmm, weird. Normally the poison only causes numbness and paralysis. It then travels to the lungs and heart if not treated."

Carter moved closer to Betha and stared at the leaves in Nalli's hand. "What are those, Parian?"

Parian gave the gargoyle a smile and then asked, "Are those Negi leaves?"

"Yes, yes. There is a healer above, but we need to get up there first," said Nalli. "I am only here because I was out gathering." Sir Samson's shoulders relaxed when she mentioned a healer.

Carter watched the two intently.

"Can you understand them?" Betha asked both Carter and Angie.

"Not a word," answered Carter.

"Nope," came from Angie.

"I wonder why I can," Betha mused.

"Starwalker, chew the leaves. They are bitter but will lessen the numbness, and the poison will stop spreading. It should be gone quickly," said Nalli. "We need to get up the mountain to a higher level, where it is safer."

Betha took the leaves and shoved one in her mouth with her good hand. Her other hand and arm felt like they weren't there anymore, and her shoulder socket was slowly losing feeling as well. The sooner her body was back to normal, the better. She still felt hot, but she wasn't panicking anymore.

She chewed another leaf, and the bitter taste made her eyes water. Nalli stared at her and said, "I know, it tastes bad, but it will help. You don't need much. Just enough."

Betha swallowed and wanted to gag. She waited a minute to see if it was going to come up. Instead, once she had swallowed, the taste faded.

"That should be good," added Nalli, taking the rest of the leaves from her. While she had been focusing on Nalli, it seemed everyone else had come to an agreement. Gargoyles jumped into the air, heading straight up.

Carter frowned. "Are we heading up as well?"

Parian turned toward Carter. "Yes. The healer is there. Plus, there are some angels above we should meet with to strategize next steps. Only one more flight."

Angie stepped out of the shadows, and several of those gathered raised weapons.

"The wolf is with us. She is bonded to the Starwalker." Sir Samson's voice was low but demanded attention. The gargoyles slowly lowered their weapons, trusting their leader's judgment.

Angie nodded her snout at Sir Samson and walked closer to Betha. *"Uh, what's next?"*

"One more flight," said Betha out loud.

Angie whined. *"Ugh, I just got my stomach settled. Is there a mountain path?"*

Betha turned toward Parian. "Is there a mountain path? Angie would rather not fly again."

Parian chuckled. "Yes, though it will take longer. If she wishes to go that way, I will go with her." Parian motioned toward the lead gargoyle and something switched with his speech. "Sir Samson, can you take Betha up? Angie is going to take the long way. Get to know the area."

Sir Samson turned toward them as Parian spoke. "It would be my honor to fly with the Starwalker." He bowed his head toward Betha.

Parian nodded at Angie. "All right, let's go the long way. I'll see if anyone else wants to join us. Carter, be careful and stretch your wings once you are up top."

Angie nudged Betha with her nose. *"I hope your arm gets healed by the time I make it to the top. See you soon."*

Sir Samson motioned for Betha to come closer. "Time to fly." He carefully scooped her up and took off toward the sky.

Betha's head felt clearer than it had since she'd gotten scratched by that demon. The air rushed over her face, and she tried to look around as they flew upward. They quickly gained height above the trees, and other gargoyles flew around them. Nalli carried the little one, Jadon, in her arms.

A gasp escaped Betha as they cleared the treetops. Rocky mountains rose behind them, but the clearing for the portal was actually halfway up the mountain that they were flying to the top of. The day was bright and clear. She could see so far. The forest ended by a wide river, and plains stretched on the other side. Smoke rose far in the distance.

Something glittered in the distance like the gold of the portal, and Betha reached out with her Traveler abilities. She could feel multiple tears—some small, some large—along with additional portals, including the one below them. Each of the openings glowed red in her mind except for the one they had used.

"Almost there, Starwalker," said Sir Samson. His voice moved her attention from the map in her mind to how far they had risen.

Betha was glad she wasn't afraid of heights. She glanced down, wondering if she could see Angie. Her friend was somewhere below climbing, which she could trace in her mind, but the trees were still covering her.

White wings flashed below them, and she spotted Carter flying upward.

"See, there is Rock Camp," said Sir Samson.

Betha glanced ahead and realized that they weren't going up anymore. Instead, they were flying straight ahead toward a clearing in the stone surrounded by short, well-guarded tents, a few campfires, and gargoyles. At least thirty people were in the small area. There were a few flashes of feathered wings, but it was hard to see much with everyone in the air.

Sir Samson landed in the clearing and set her down on her feet. They were quickly surrounded by more gargoyles, all talking at once. Some stared at her. White wings moved through the crowd, which parted to let an angel make his way toward her.

"What happened to your arm?" asked the angel.

Without asking for permission, the guy laid a hand on her shoulder and muttered in an almost song-like way. Warmth flowed from his hand down her arm and into her fingers. The difference in temperature caused her to flinch and bite down on her tongue to keep from whimpering. With all of the eyes on her, she did her best not to panic. It felt like fire. Painful fire.

Yet, as the fire receded, feeling returned down her

arm and to her fingertips. The angel pulled away, shaking his head. "That should be better. Freaking demonic monkeys—always getting someone in a group. You shouldn't have been able to move right now. The poison usually takes effect much more quickly. The fates work in mysterious ways, I guess."

His rambling continued, but she felt Carter land nearby. He moved right behind her, and the other angel stepped backward at Carter's presence.

"Are you okay?" he asked near her ear.

Betha nodded and took a step back, away from the unknown angel.

"This way, Starwalker," said Sir Samson. "We have tent and fire for you." He turned toward Nalli. "Let the elders know she is here, and we will meet soon. There are too many people in this camp. Send a group to the hold."

Nalli nodded, but her lips drew tight in a line.

Sir Samson moved through the talking crowd, and Betha picked up several words, including Starwalker, portals, and elders. Nalli moved in a different direction and called for attention. Thankfully, the crowd lessened as Betha followed Sir Samson closer to the tents and the campfires. The tall rocks blocked some of the airflow, but if the wind had been blowing, she would bet money that it would be very cold up here.

They approached one of the fires, which was surrounded by three gargoyles leaning in toward the flames. They were talking, but too low for her to make out. Each had strands of wooden beads and stones hanging down their chests. It reminded her of the ones

Sir Samson and Derrik had, but these were more complex.

Sir Samson motioned to the fire and the figures. "Starwalker, these are elders." He spoke in English to her. She wasn't sure if that was annoyance she heard from him. It was clear he didn't expect them to be here.

"Why are you talking to her like that? Use our language. She should know it," said a female elder.

He turned back toward her with a frown, and his voice changed. "Can you understand our tongue?"

Betha blushed. "Once we came through the portal, it started to make sense."

Carter gasped behind her. "You just spoke their language."

"The true Starwalkers always could understand others," answered a different elder. He gave her a bright smile. "Come sit at our fire. We will have food brought. You have that tent as well. We need to welcome and thank you for joining us."

Carter gave her a nod and headed toward the tent. To her surprise, Derrik followed with the bags that they had been carrying. She reached out to Angie across the mountain and could feel her getting closer. A bright ball of joy was coming from her so Betha withdrew. She didn't want to interrupt Angie's run up the mountain.

Betha moved forward and sat down next to Sir Samson on a log. The heat coming off of the flames felt amazing, especially on the hand she had lost feeling in. She stretched her fingers toward it.

"We are the elders of the gargoyle clans," said the female elder. "I am Talli from the plains, this is Gero from the far mountains, and this is Bedson from the hold." She pointed to each of the elders beside her as she spoke their names. Gero had a ridge on his forehead and was a deep gray, while Bedson was very similar looking to Sir Samson with dark hair. Talli had blue paint across her face in a pattern that was very much like the paint Nalli wore. "We welcome you to our fire on the mountain. Though this is a time of blood and not celebration. In these times, our clans have shrunk, and we are now only one." Her sentence seemed to shake Sir Samson, who sat beside her. His eyes grew wide as he glanced between the three of them, though he did not speak.

Betha felt like she needed to introduce herself. "I am Betha, a Traveler, though Sir Samson calls me a Starwalker. I am sorry for your losses."

Gero's deep voice spoke up, "It is our penance for not doing our duty." He bowed his head. "We turned our backs on the Starwalkers, and now we beg for your help. We let the Guardians fade after settling these lands, and now we suffer. I hope the bloodshed is sacrifice enough and you will help us."

All three bowed their heads toward her, waiting for a response.

"I feel like I am missing something here," said Betha. She turned toward Sir Samson, whose head was also bowed. "Who are the Guardians?"

Bedson's head rose. "The ones who guard the portals of course. Our forefathers let the practice lapse, and now the demons stream in for blood."

"Wait, how do Guardians guard the portals?" What she knew was that *Travelers* guarded the portals. Or at least that was what she'd been told. This wasn't making sense.

"When one has passed the trials set before him or her and been declared fit, they then bond to a portal. They are lost to us, but they can protect the portal from misuse. My brother guards the one below," said Sir Samson. He peered into the fire.

"What do you mean they are lost?"

Sir Samson shook his head. "They are no more, they vanish. As a chief, my brother made the decision to sacrifice himself to protect it when we realized our mistake. Those who mean to wage war cannot cross." The map rose back to her mind. Each of the portals or tears glowed red except for the one below. It was white, almost blue. "We lost his wife and daughter. He did it to protect our people and his son." The wings on the conference room table made more sense, and she wanted to throw up.

"Will you help us?" asked Talli.

"Of course. I came all this way to help. I can close the tears that don't belong, which will help stem the flow of demons. There are so many ways they can slip through. That will reduce the numbers here."

The three elders nodded in relief and Talli smiled at Betha. "You have our thanks. The angel host is fighting in the south, though the plains have also been attacked. We have lost many. My home is still free, and we are holding it with all of our hearts," said Talli.

"Derrik has passed his trials, and we are hoping more will follow. Right now, we can't get anyone near the portals to make the bonds," added Gero.

Her eyes landed on Derrik, who was standing next to the tent near Carter. He gave her a nod.

"I can close the tears. I just need to get near them and I have an idea of how I can get to them. Then if we can clear out the demons, he will have plenty of time to do what he needs to do with the portals that belong."

The maps of all of the different portals and tears came to mind. This was going to take some time. The number was staggering. Plus, how was Derrik going to bond with a portal? Betha needed more information about all of this, but the Elders had either told her all they knew, or all they were prepared to share. They seemed to think she should know things, as a Starwalker, but she didn't, and had no idea where she might learn.

THIS FOREST SMELLED MUCH MORE similar to the forests on Pack land. The trail was rough under Angie's paws, and she could tell that this pathway wasn't used very often. Not to mention the boulders that she had to creep over at times. A shadow flickered overhead when the trees cleared, but every time she glanced upward, it was that angel, Parian.

Freaking flying people. Protecting others from flying creatures wasn't something she was good at. Her training had not prepared her to defend against things coming from above.

Her wolves senses plus the bond led her toward the camp. She knew how far away Betha and Carter were, and she was excited to get to them. Her wolf forced her attention back to the trail—these scents would be important if they would be patrolling the ground. That brought up the fact that she didn't know if any of the demons flew, and she wondered if the gargoyles were keeping guard of the camp well enough. Parian flying overhead could see the trail here and there, but what about the underbrush?

Angie darted into one shadow and came out further ahead on the trail. Her nose worked overtime trying to catch any sulfur or static on the air currents. Did the other camps have a ground patrol, or were the demons winning the ground game, so to speak?

Her brain was going in way too many directions, and she reached out to Carter. *"Not many people use this trail. Do they do ground patrols? Or are they only flying? There should be rounds this way if the camp is as close as you are in my head."*

"You aren't smelling any ground patrols?" asked Carter.

"Not at all," Angie slowed down from her run and began to sniff around even more. The camp had to be very close. The shadow above passed her, then circled back. *"I can search more."*

"Is everything okay?" asked Parian from above. He was flying in place, which seemed very impressive to the wolf.

Angie nodded and tried to wiggle her snout. She did not want to shift into her human form. Instead, she motioned with her nose and then started walking slowly in the correct direction.

"Are you smelling for trouble?"

Angie nodded.

"Do you smell anything right now?"

She shook her snout no, which was harder than she thought it would be.

"Okay, that's good," said Parian. He rose back in the air. "Howl if you smell anything."

"I forgot how nice it is to speak to ya'll in wolf form," sent Angie.

"Sorry, though I bet Parian can figure out what you are doing," replied Carter.

Angie continued up the trail, this time going slower but still not smelling anything interesting. No demons but also no gargoyles. This was dangerous. What if they had no ground patrols anywhere? She had noticed Derrik didn't seem very happy on the ground, but this was a crazy lapse in judgment. She prayed she didn't smell anything out of place the rest of the way up the mountain.

TEN

Betha felt better after sleeping, though she was pretty sure that the day and night cycle was not twenty-four hours here. It felt closer to thirty. The night had lasted longer than she felt was normal, and now the sun was finally peeking over the horizon and into the tent. It was a roomy space that the three of them were sharing. She had no clue what material it was made out of. It had been the biggest tent she had noticed last night.

"They have two moons," commented Angie.

"Did you go out last night?" asked Betha.

"Of course," said Angie. "I wandered through the camp, staying hidden, and I checked out the surrounding forest and trails. I know you trust these gargoyles, but I wanted to make sure that things were as presented."

Carter shook his head with a smirk, pulling on his gear. "Did you find anything new?"

Angie frowned. "No, it seems to be as they said it was. Derrik did some weird dance around a fire when the moons were high in the sky. The elders also painted symbols on his chest. They, well, they remind me of our tattoos."

That was an interesting fact, and Betha wondered if Derrik would show the symbols to her. Then again, given his chest hadn't been covered on the journey here, she should be able to get a good look.

"No sign of demons nearby, but everyone was definitely on guard. Things are tense. Lots of low talking that I couldn't make out. There aren't very many angels here. Only that healer, Parian, and someone who left at dawn."

"How is your arm feeling?" asked Carter. He moved closer to look at it, and Betha held it up.

"You can touch it—it's fine. Feels like normal except my fingers are a little stiff. The cut healed, though it looks like it might scar."

He ran his hands over her shoulder and down to her elbow. Betha did her best not to turn bright red. "Here, let's stretch it out." Carter then directed her arm in several different positions. "I had to do a ton of PT after I manifested. Running through some stretches would be good. We don't want it to seize up."

"I appreciate it."

Angie's voice whispered across her mind. "*You are bright red, but it might be a good moment to say something.*" Her dark-haired friend gave her a wink before heading outside the tent, giving them privacy.

"Carter," whispered Betha. But her voice caught on what she really wanted to say. She cleared her throat and tried again. "Thank you for joining us on this adventure."

"Of course—we are anchored." He lightly bent her

fingers back, and Betha would bet money even her ears were red. His hands were warm on her skin, and it felt great.

"I mean, maybe when we are back on Terra, we should grab some food together." She hesitated. "Alone, I mean. Well us, you know, you and me, but no one else?" This was not going well. Not at all.

"We should do that." He paused for a moment, like he was thinking of how to reply. "It would be good to get to know you better." His hands moved her wrist in a slow circle. "I can't believe I didn't know you were a coffee addict."

Betha blinked. "Hey, there is nothing wrong with a good cup of coffee."

"Speaking of coffee," said Angie as she came back into the tent. She had the thermos that Betha had been carrying on the trip there. "I made you instant coffee using what I had left."

"Oh, thank the fates—you are amazing!"

Carter let go of her wrist. "That should be enough for now. We'll want to repeat that before you go to bed tonight."

Betha took the thermos carefully and took a small sip of the hot beverage. While the coffee was only okay, it was a touchpoint for home that made her smile.

"What would I do without you?" asked Betha.

Angie turned away with a shrug. "You would be fine, just a little less caffeinated. The gargoyles are cooking over the fires and seem to be gearing up. I could use a translator—turns out, most do not speak our language. Or only a few easy words."

"Speaking of that, it is a weird experience. I have no idea how I know what they're saying."

"I mean, you also *spoke* it yesterday," added Carter.

"I don't understand how that's possible."

"Shouldn't you be more like, thank the fates? It's going to make our time here much easier. I didn't even imagine that we wouldn't understand each other," said Angie.

The ramifications of traveling to a different world hadn't really hit Betha either. "Somehow, I hadn't thought about the practical things like time differences, language barriers, and different technology. Of course different worlds would be different." For whatever reason, she had assumed that things would be like Terra. Now that she thought about it, things couldn't be like Terra everywhere, but it just hadn't ever occurred to her.

"At least we can each fight with swords," said Carter. He looked at Angie. "Or claws. I thank the fates for that. You can't cross portals with technology. Electronics fry, and gunpowder doesn't work. It has something to do with energy density. I don't understand it, but at least we have our swords."

"Let's do this," said Betha before she headed outside of the tent. For some reason she expected things to be super busy. Yet, the camp was rather quiet. There were tents, but fewer than what she remembered last night. Three different campfires were burning, and some gargoyles were silently watching the skies.

Sir Samson sat near the fire right outside the large tent she was staying in. Angie sat near him on a log, and he handed her something on a plate. It looked edible.

"May the dawn greet you, Starwalker." His voice was deep, and he sipped on a warm beverage. The air was cooler than she thought it would be, but the sun was just coming over the horizon. "I hoped to see you this morning before I am off."

Betha approached the fire and gave him a smile. "Where are you heading?"

"Back to the south. The fighting is centered there. We are holding for now. I was wondering what *your* plan is. This is a small camp protecting the portal below. It is safe. The elders are staying here instead of going to Mountain Hold. The little ones and families left for Mountain Hold last night. More should go, but the—"

"The remaining members of the Plains Clan are stubborn," said Talli as she exited the tent across the way. "We will hold onto our home as long as we can." Talli bared her teeth at Sir Samson.

"The little ones should leave."

"We will hold." Talli's voice was firm.

Betha did not want to interrupt that conversation, but Angie gave her a nod.

"What's the plan, Betha?" asked Angie. Inside her head, she continued, "*What the heck are they saying?*" Betha quickly gave them both a mental recap. She could feel Carter roll his eyes from inside the tent. His disagreement with Talli's assessment echoed Betha's, but it wasn't her place.

"I am going to focus on the tears that I can reach from this portal and work my way south. It should give me a good feel for what's going on," said Betha.

Angie nodded, and Betha realized she had spoken in

her own language. Sir Samson grinned, but Talli looked confused. He quickly translated to the elder.

"I am going to try to go in-between to do it," added Betha.

"I mean, it will be safe for you," said Angie. "I like it. We can operate from this portal. Carter and I can protect this area. Just don't vanish for weeks at a time."

Betha shrugged. "I didn't know that had happened last time. That's not really up to me."

Carter exited the tent with both his bag and hers. "It's a good plan. I can work on flying, and Angie can cover the trails below."

"If you guard here, I'll send the portal guards south," said Sir Samson in their tongue. Talli glanced back and forth between the group, and clearly trying to follow the conversation.

"You need to eat something," said Angie to Betha. "And then we can head to the portal below."

Now that she was standing in front of the portal to the desert world, Betha had doubts.

"*You got this,*" whispered Angie. The giant wolf was sitting on her haunches right next to her. She had opted to go the trail route again. When Betha had mentioned getting a ride flying down, Angie had stated a hard no. Betha had gotten a ride down with Derrik. It hadn't been as smooth as the rides with Sir Samson, and she wondered if Derrik was used to flying with someone. While she had noticed something painted on his chest, she hadn't taken the time to study it. Yet, she had felt something in her mind map when she touched it. Betha didn't understand it, but now it was time for her to do her thing. She could figure out strange gargoyle rituals later.

Betha, Carter, and Angie stood in front of the portal. Betha had on her armor and her sword, which made her look more impressive than she felt. Derrik flew above, scouting for any trouble. When Sir Samson had left, Derrik had stayed behind. It had something to do with sticking near her in case he could bond with a portal. While she had so many questions about that, they were on hold. Step one was making sure she could do what she thought she could.

"I packed your bag with a few things in case this goes sideways," said Carter. He motioned to the pack at his feet. It did look less full than when she had last carried it. She reached for the pack and swung it up on her shoulders.

"I don't know how long I will be gone. I only plan to close a few nearby tears. This world is riddled with them. I don't understand it." Betha shook her head lightly. "I don't know how time will change. I'm hoping it's more like two hours versus two days."

"Be careful and take your time. Don't rush things. We will be here when you get back," said Carter. He patted her shoulder lightly.

Betha smirked. "All right, here I go yet again."

"*I mean, it's your thing,*" rang across the mental bond from Angie. "*You go through portals.*"

Betha couldn't help the chuckle that came to her lips

at the matter-of-fact statement, and she entered the portal, smiling.

The world turned dark, and lights appeared in the sky. Now Betha understood it wasn't a night sky with stars but rather various doorways that led to other worlds. Fireflies appeared as she took a step forward. The pathway lit up, going off into the distance.

Betha turned to face the doorway she had come through. It wasn't white. Instead, it glowed a soft blue, and it felt different. She reached out with her abilities to see what it felt like.

"You are a Starwalker," whispered a masculine voice. "Have you come to help us?"

Betha blinked and then realized it was coming from the doorway. "Yes. Are you Sir Samson's brother?" She took a step closer to the portal. Fireflies rose around the doorway.

"Yes. He succeeded then. I knew when Samson left and then came back with others, but they meant no harm, so I let them through. It is good you are here—our people will survive this."

"I am going to heal the barrier between your world and the hells."

The voice did not respond, and the fireflies drifted away from the doorway. Betha looked toward the right side of the portal. When she had been in Sky World, there had been several tears in that direction, all of which had glowed red.

"I am looking for the tears," whispered Betha to the fireflies. They seemed to hover and then they moved toward the right. Betha carefully veered off of the glowing path, and a stepping stone formed for her. Feeling more confident, she took the next step. The stones appeared with each step she took, so she tried to ignore them. And the emptiness below her feet.

The first tear wasn't far, and she studied it for a moment. This was a natural tear, but it had been stretched. Betha had discovered and closed a natural tear on Terra, and they felt different from the ones that the knife had created. She could tell this one was used to cross the world because it was rimmed in tinges of red, although it wasn't dripping like the ones on Terra had been. Drawing her power to the edge was quicker than she thought it would be, and the tear closed almost instantly. She pulled her hand away in shock.

"Maybe since someone wasn't using it, it was easier," she mumbled to herself. The fireflies danced nearby. "Can you lead me to more like this?"

They moved off quicker this time, as if they now understood what she was looking for. The next was smaller than the first, and it felt like it wasn't used as much. There wasn't any red with it. Instead, it was an off-white color. It closed even quicker by barely touching it. The pattern continued after this. Close a tear and move on to the next one.

Then one was different—a knife had been used to create it. That must be what the knife had been used for before the prince brought it to Terra. It felt the same as the ones he'd cut on Terra, yet it was much older. This one was used frequently. Red outlined the edges, and the closer she got, the more she could feel a dull ache in her chest. Betha frowned. This wouldn't do.

"All right, time to fix this one."

Her power came as she called for it, but it was much harder. Betha pulled more to herself, bright light flickering over her hands in the darkness. She could feel beings using the portal. The image of various demons screaming flashed in front of her eyes, and she yanked even harder.

"This is going to heal!"

Bright white light streamed from her fingertips, smothering the red and drawing it closed. Finally, it snapped shut. She breathed hard, and sweat dripped down her back, but the ache in her chest was gone. Betha turned back the way she had come.

"I need a break after that," she said to herself, or to the emptiness—she wasn't entirely sure.

Each step she had taken glowed in the darkness. The walk back to the portal seemed to take much longer than the walk to where she was. Finally, she was in front of the blueish doorway. Betha touched the edge of it and slipped through. Inside her mind, she heard a whisper, *"By the way, my name is Magson."*

The clearing rose before her, and a giant wolf jumped at the sight of her coming through the portal. Betha crashed to her knees, her hands shaking. The sky was darkening, and her stomach growled. She had heard him in her mind when she had touched the portal. That was new.

"Yep, definitely time for a break," she said.

～

THE FIRST ROUND of healing on Sky World was done. Betha was thankful to be sitting on a log next to the campfire. Some sort of meat stew bubbled over the fire, and she had already eaten one bowl. The meat wasn't one she recognized, but something like potatoes were in it. Concern radiated down the bond, urging her to eat more. The flames flickered in the darkness, and stars were doing a show in the sky. This wasn't bad. Not at all.

"So, what happened?" asked Angie. She sat across the fire from Betha, her notebook in hand. Betha was pretty sure Angie was sketching the campsite. She'd loved drawing forever, but Betha knew she hadn't had time to nurture her gift in a long time. It was good to see her get into it again. Hopefully, someday Angie could be a professional artist. But first, things would have to calm down.

"To be honest, it wasn't bad until I got to the last one. It wasn't a natural tear. Tears are like...the barrier was worn down and so it tore. The last one was *created*, and it wasn't new," said Betha. The knife seemed to get warm when she was thinking about the tear since she had come back from closing it. Yet for the moment, she was keeping it in the boot. It needed to remain hidden. A big part of her hoped it had been this knife, and they weren't dealing with a different one. It had felt like it probably was. "I didn't realize that healing an older tear would be substantially harder. Demons were actively using it as well."

"Do you know where?" The question was soft and came from Derrik, who was perched on a boulder. He watched over the area in the darkness.

Betha shook her head. "I didn't want to poke my head through." She motioned to Angie. "Angie would have then been able to sense me and know where I was, but anyone near the portal could potentially see me. It seemed like a bad idea." Not to mention, she hadn't thought of it at the time.

"I can't even guess how far away it was—space isn't the same there as here. Or at least I hope so since it wasn't too far of a walk. Also, time itself passes differently. Based on my internal clock, I had only been gone for four hours or so, while it was actually closer to late afternoon here."

Angie's pencil moved across the page, and the tip reflected in the firelight. "Mission accomplished. You closed a whole bunch of tears, one of which was an active supply line. This was a successful day. Tomorrow will be as well. Now you need to eat, drink, and rest some more."

"What she said," commented Carter. He walked out from behind one of the tents. Sweat dripped down his forehead. From what Betha gathered, he had been working with the gargoyles left behind. Fighting in the air was harder or something. Either way, today did feel like a good day, and Angie was right. It was a great first step. Consistency was going to be key. Each day, she would need to close more tears.

Behind her eyelids, she focused on the map she had of the portals and tears across this world. It was different now. But it wasn't like she had cleared one section and could move on to the next. Space wasn't linear in the in-between. She also noticed a flicker on the map, right near them. When she opened her eyes, she realized that it was Derrik.

"Hey Derrik, can I see your chest?" asked Betha. She hoped that had come out in the correct language.

He jumped off of the boulder and walked closer to the fire. A necklace draped down across his chest, and Betha realized how much taller he was than her. His skin was dark, but it wasn't all one color. The closer he got, the more she realized different tones were woven throughout. Lilac was mixed in with the grays.

"It means I have been accepted to bond with a portal. The symbols help with the bonding." His long fingers pulled the necklace aside, and he stood next to her. Betha quickly stood up, as the large gargoyle definitely had a different opinion of personal space.

The artwork had to have been done with a paintbrush, and it fit with what Angie had mentioned. It was a bright blue color with very thin lines. The compass rose was the main design, and surrounding it were maybe wings. Betha wasn't sure. It reminded her of the wings surrounding her own marking, which she held up in the firelight—feathers flared out from it instead of the wings which were on his chest.

"It looks like one of our markings. Carter and Angie have them. How does it provide help?"

Derrek shrugged. "The elders say it helps the portal connect with us easier. Magson's bonding took a long time. This might make it not so."

"Can I touch it?"

He nodded and stood as still as a statue. She reached out and poked it with her pointer finger. It didn't feel different than his skin. Yet, behind her eyelids, he flickered. It wasn't like her Anchors, yet it was similar. He wasn't hers. Betha didn't understand why they would paint an anchored symbol on his chest when he wasn't anchored. She needed to speak to the elders, but they had left. It was like they didn't want her to change her mind so they fled before she could.

"It is a great honor to have been chosen for the trials, and to have succeeded. It has taken many years, and I bring honor to my family," said Derrik. He sounded sad, despite his words.

"Why does it sound like you aren't happy about it?" asked Betha.

"I am proud to be able to serve. But I am the only one chosen so far, and that means I cannot fight. I watch my people die, and I cannot help them until I can get to a portal and bond with it. The demons have control near the two other ones. So I watch much pain and must bear that, too. It is difficult, Starwalker."

Betha rested her hand on Derrik's chest. "I am sure when the time comes, you will make your people proud, Derrik," she said at last. The tall gargoyle only nodded, then stepped away, going back to his lonely watch on the stone.

Angie watched Betha across the fire in between strokes of her pencil. Drawing brought her so much joy, but she didn't have a ton of time to practice. Several years ago, she had thought one day she might be an artist. When she had discovered Betha had asked Carter to fit a notepad and a few pencils in one of the bags, she had been overjoyed. Now it gave her something to do instead of being right next to Betha in her personal space.

When Betha had come back through the portal, she had looked like shit. Her face was white, she was covered in sweat, and her eyes stared off into space. Not to mention it was a whole ten or so hours later. Her wolf could only stand so much pacing. Or running through the forest.

Carter was working on that flying thing with Derrik, and she knew what most of the scents were in the surrounding forests. Now Betha was talking in the gargoyle language like she was born to it. Then again, it seemed like she was. Angie had peered at Derrik's mark already. It was very close to what was on her chest, only she had shadows surrounding her star. It was strange. Angie didn't know what to make of it. Or this whole situation. The gargoyles acted like Betha was their savior, but the elders had left as soon as Derrik had been marked.

A war was going on, so she could understand them leaving to help. It just didn't sit right with her. Something felt off. Angie wished she could go with Betha. At least then her friend would be safe.

CHAPTER

ELEVEN

The morning was turning out to be more rage inducing than anticipated. The king's orders sinking into her brain made the princess want to scream. He was the only one higher than her in the hierarchy, and therefore the only one who could command her so. Even still, every time it happened, Akeldama wanted to kill him. The loss of free will wasn't something she had ever learned to deal with. Other demons didn't have a problem with it, and part of her wondered if it was because she was a royal.

Each step further away from him helped her relax, calming down, letting her bottle up the rage inside and keep it hidden. She didn't need anyone seeing a break in her armor or an opportunity to take her down. Staying on top was everything. All she had done until this point was to prove her place as heir. Akeldama had to prove she had enough power, not just the right blood. Someday she was going to be queen, hopefully sooner rather than later with how the king was going. The trip through the portal to her lands made it easier to breathe. The second level of hell was her own.

"Bring this Traveler to my camp," bounced around inside her head, but the pressure was substantially less now. She would do as ordered, and it might already be done. The lieutenant that she had sent off should be reporting back to her soon. That was one benefit of having Typhon answer to her—he could fast travel across the hells, teleporting nearly instantly between any two points on one of the worlds they claimed as their own. Her brother had never realized his potential. Or the fact that he was her spy. From what she had learned, it was clear the prince was inept. With her brother's death, the bonds he'd had with lower demons had broken. She was recruiting only the best and brightest of his troops, since so many of them were barely fit to serve as meat.

Hopefully Typhon had good news for her. He was already on the balcony when she entered. Akeldama couldn't help the smile that came across her face as her eyes trailed over his broad shoulders. Typhon was tall, muscular, and bright. All traits that she cherished in her followers. Not to mention he was pretty to look at. The way his hair fell into his eyes always struck a chord. His ability to literally pick her up made her heart flutter. Typhon turned quickly at the sound of her feet on the stone. His amber eyes touched hers, then he bowed his head.

"How did it go?" she asked.

Typhon's head stayed down, and her frustration rose. "The Traveler was hit by one of the Piccum demons, and the whole group quickly fled to the sky. We weren't expecting so many flyers. They made it to the portal for the potential Seventh Circle, but we could not follow. The portal was protected somehow."

Her anger flared, and her fingers glowed for a moment, then she froze. "The portal was protected?" The princess studied him. "What do you mean protected?"

"We could not pass, no matter what. The portal was there, but we could not cross."

Portals could be protected. This was new to her. A shiver went up her spine, and Akeldama didn't suppress it. This wasn't good news, but if she had it first, it would be an advantage. "Who else knows about this?"

"No one. I removed the others." His voice was low, and he flashed his sharp teeth.

Akeldama gave him a soft smile and moved closer. Her fingers trailed up his arm. "You have pleased me. We can work with this."

Ideas rolled around inside her head. If portals could be protected, then separating the king from the rest of the hells could be done. His power would be reduced if he couldn't access the lands. Being in the Sixth Hell was hard enough for the ruler—he kept having to travel back to the Fourth since the Sixth was not fully under his control. After the prince died, she had already taken over the Third Circle, and her own power had grown. The number of demons she could now hold under her command had more than doubled.

Maybe it was time to look at the Fifth Circle and see if she could break the king's hold on it. The Fifth Circle was empty, barren. Past rulers had looted it of all resources. It was now a crossroads of sorts. It connected the Sixth

Circle, the Fey Wilds, and the Second Circle, which was hers. The war with the gargoyles was taking its own toll on the king's troops, and support from the families of hell was reaching its limit. Add in the trouble the prince had caused where so many demons had been slaughtered on Terra, and the number of troops under her father's direct control was shrinking by the day.

Typhon twitched under her fingertips, snapping her back to the present. *"Bring this Traveler to my camp,"* pushed again against her mind. "I need to retrieve the Traveler for the king. Send out scouts to find her location. I have a present that should help take care of the wolf and angel. And maybe something else that interests you."

Heat rose in his eyes, and she smiled in return. This afternoon would be much more pleasant than anticipated.

THIS TIME, the in-between seemed to be expecting her. Betha was on a mission. More tears needed to close, which would clean up the map in her mind. This world had so many tears and portals, her mental map was a mess of red slashes of wounds in the fabric of the world. Not to mention the solid portals, one of which she knew went to the angelic world. That was how the angels were getting to Sky World. It was toward the south, where a large part of the fighting was. It was clear the demons were trying to force the angels back to the portal.

The fireflies welcomed her, and before she could ask

anything, they darted off in a different direction. They led her quickly to one tear. It was another natural tear, but it was older and had been used recently. It closed quickly and then they were off again. Today she could move quickly between them, and the steps in the darkness almost appeared before she decided where she was going to step.

Then something dawned on her. "Are you encouraging me to move faster?" Her voice was soft in the space, and her glowing friends danced in place in response. That could be a yes, but Betha wasn't sure. Either way, they were leading her to certain tears, all of which had been used and were connected to the demonic realm.

Betha followed them to the next tear, which glowed a dull red. Instantly she knew this was created by a knife, and it was old. Probably the oldest tear she had come across. The edges were dulled like the edges of scarred tissue instead of a fresh cut. It felt like this tear was frequently used. Betha touched the edge of it and instead of directly trying to close it, she tried to see out into the gargoyles world. Her head spun, then things slowly took shape.

Grassland spread out before her with low bushes. If this was Terra, she would say they were berry bushes. Angels fought in the skies in the distance against other flying shapes. Creatures roamed in the bushes, but she couldn't make out what they were.

"*Betha?*" asked Angie's voice.

"*All good, just peeking.*"

"*You are really far south.*"

Given that the sun rose high overhead, it wasn't late in the day yet. *"Okay, going to close this."* Betha yanked away from the tear and stumbled backward in the darkness. She landed on her rear, and everything spun. Her stomach heaved, but she resisted the urge. Throwing up in the in-between was not going to happen.

Minutes ticked by, and when she opened her eyes, she was covered in fireflies.

"I am okay, that was just...unsettling."

The fireflies slowly peeled away, and she climbed to her feet, not focusing on the fact that the only floor she had was what she was touching. The tear loomed in front of her, and she touched the edges. This time she brought forth her power which glowed brightly in the darkness. It shot out of her hands and darted across the opening, landing on the edge farthest away from her. With a yank, it snapped shut.

Betha stared at the place the tear had been, wondering what had just happened. Her power hadn't ever reacted like that before. She wasn't shaky, no sweat, and she felt fine. It was strange.

The fireflies danced and tried to lead her forward. "All right, let's do another." They darted off into the darkness, and she followed.

Betha stumbled out of Magson's portal when it was still early afternoon. She felt like she was getting the hang of this. The map behind her eyelids had cleaned up substantially. Instead of the world near her being a complete crisscross pattern of red, it was now readable. The portal behind her glowed faintly blue, and another one glowed bright white in the distance to the south. Close by that portal were two others glowing bright red. This world did not have as many connections to other worlds as Terra.

"*You are back early,*" said Angie. Her friend nudged her with her snout.

"*The more I close, the easier it seems to get, I think. Less sure on that than I would like.*" Betha pushed an image of the map inside her head to her friend. "*It is so much better than when I started. It feels like the more I close, the clearer the map is, like there was too much activity to get a good feel on it.*"

"*Are those four big ones actual portals?*" asked Angie.

"*Yep, the rest are tears. Some natural, some not.*"

Derrik landed in the clearing. "Carter said you had appeared. Are you ready to head back to camp?" He was her designated carrier, bringing her back and forth since Carter was still working on strengthening his wings. Not to mention, Betha felt sure she would blush herself to death if Carter were the one to carry her.

Betha studied the map in her mind. Based on what she had cleaned up already, it should only take two or three more days to finish up. "How is the fighting going?"

Derrik shrugged. "A messenger should be headed this way soon, then on to Mountain Hold."

"I could probably do another round. I will keep it short. No more than four or five," she promised.

"Are you sure that's a good idea?" called down Carter.

A shadow flew overhead, and she waved. "We don't want you to push it. It's better to be safe."

"*What he said,*" added Angie. "*You don't know how much time will pass. Plus you were really far away when you peeked through that portal.*"

Betha could feel the hesitancy coming off of Angie. Her big black wolf looked calm as could be, but inside, her friend wasn't as confident.

"All right, how about three? I'll be quick, I promise." The giant wolf rolled her eyes at her, and Betha gave her a smirk before she let it drop. " I could see the fighting in the distance from that one portal. I don't think it's going well."

She waved at Carter, who was still flying overhead. "Derrik, I'll be back soon. Just a little more work for today." The image of the angel fighting the flying shapes came to mind. While they were hanging out here, people were in a war in the south.

Betha turned back to the portal and headed into the darkness.

"Going again?" asked a voice.

"Yes, Magson. The sooner I heal the tears, the sooner Sky World will be safe."

There wasn't a response, so she turned to the fireflies that had appeared. "Can you keep me closer to this portal than all the way down south?"

She wasn't sure if they had understood her request, but they led her to a few tears back-to-back. The first three were easy, natural tears that had been used, but not heavily.

"I can do one more, then I need to head back."

This one seemed very close to where she had already been working. It was smaller than most of the others. Yet, the edges were a deep red. Betha stared at it, trying to figure out what made this one different. It was smaller, but used heavily, and used recently. Almost as much use as the much older tear from this morning. It didn't make sense.

Decisively, she touched the edges and tried to peek through. It was smoky, but it didn't look like anyone was around.

"Mama!"

Betha's eyes grew wide at the sound.

"Betha, what are you doing?" asked Carter.

"Something isn't right."

"You aren't that far away."

"There is a child crying..." her voice trailed off as another sound came. This time she recognized the voice.

"You need to run, child! I can't fly you away. Go north!" Parian's voice rolled across the smoke.

"Mama!"

"You have to be quiet, little one!"

"Parian is here. Something is wrong." Betha pushed more of herself through the tear to the gargoyle world. Her feet landed on the rocky ground. A scream made her turn.

"Oh, fuck."

Demons were on the other side of the opening to hell. They charged at her. Betha touched the tear and yanked with everything she had. It snapped shut, cutting off the pathway.

"Betha! I'm coming! Don't you dare get hurt." Angie's

voice was a chant in her mind, and she could feel two dots moving quickly toward her location. Instead of staying put, she yanked out her sword and ran to a section of underbrush nearby.

"Parian," whispered Betha. She needed to find the angel and the child. The underbrush cleared, and Betha could see the source of the smoke. The clearing contained blackened husks of what looked to be huts. Charred wood smoked in distinct piles. Fallen gargoyles and an angel lay surrounded by blood.

She crept forward, trying to listen for anything. Finally, she heard someone inside one of the partially collapsed huts. "Parian?"

"Betha?"

Betha moved cautiously near the hut, and her fingers tightened on her sword. Parian was inside, one of his wings broken. It dragged on the ground. His bright white feathers were dirty and sprinkled with blood.

"You need to take the child and go. I can give you some time. Let Rock Camp know the demons are attacking across the plains. I was on my way to deliver an update. They need to let Mountain Hold know. The plains are falling. We can't hold the demons back."

The glowing presence of her anchors moved closer, faster now. The child in Parian's arms was silent, her wings wrapped close around her body. Her dark green eyes stared at Betha in awe. Or maybe shock.

"I don't know where the demons are coming from, but it's close," said Parian.

"I closed the tear—they aren't getting here anymore." She checked behind her eyelids and realized there weren't any other tears nearby. "Reinforcements aren't coming from anywhere close anyway." Betha moved closer to Parian to try to see what could be done with his wing.

"It can't be saved as is." His voice was only a whisper, but Betha heard it clear as day. Sounds of something moving through the trees from the opposite direction of Rock Camp reached her. She turned, gripping her sword tighter.

"Angie and Carter are on their way. They will be here shortly."

"You need to go," he pled as he held the child. "Take the child and go. Tell my son I love him."

Anger rolled through her as she looked at the bodies in between the huts. So many dead and for what? What could possibly be worth this?

"*We hit a few demons,*" said Carter.

Betha hadn't even realized that they had stopped moving. Her focus was opposite them on something moving through the underbrush, heading in their direction. Parian and the child remained huddled in the hut behind her.

"You will see your son again," said Betha. She stepped into what must have been a gathering square. Two sides were open to the bushes and trees. A pair of red glowing eyes stared at her from the leaves. Her sword was ready.

A demon dashed out into the open, stretching to pounce. Betha steadied herself, pulling at everything she knew. Still, anger rocked her. How dare these demons try to take yet another world? How dare they kill and hurt so many?

Then it was right in front of her. With bright red eyes, it looked like a lynx from Terra but with scales instead of fur. Fire gathered in its mouth as it jumped at her over a fallen gargoyle. Betha screamed and held up her sword. White light rushed down her sword, and she rolled to the side. Heat washed over her, then vanished.

The demon screamed in terror—one touch was all it took. Betha didn't watch, instead looking back to the underbrush. She could hear more coming. This wasn't over.

CHAPTER

TWELVE

Fiery anger kept her steady. Her biggest concern was to keep moving. She was fast. Not as fast as Angie, but still faster than most would expect. Her sword wasn't glowing anymore, but she knew the angel fire was right there. Waiting. Right under the surface.

Another beast dashed out in the open, heading straight toward her. Another slunk over to one side. Given the fire she had seen in the demon's mouth, this was concerning. Again, Betha waited. She might only have a few tricks up her sleeve, but she knew how to use them. Carter had drilled them into her head. Nick it and then move. The angel fire would take care of the rest.

The one heading toward her ran faster than the last, but her sword came up, and she rolled in the opposite direction. It was hard to keep her sword away from her body as she rolled. Fire shot in her direction but was then cut off as something dark slammed into the demon's body.

Angie growled, then vanished. Something happened

134

in the bushes where the demons had come from. Carter landed beside her, his own sword out and glowing.

"Where is Parian?" he asked.

"I am here," said Parian, crawling out from the shadows in the broken hut. "You need to cauterize my wound."

Betha crawled to her feet. "Help Parian I'll keep watch."

CARTER FLEW EVEN FASTER than when Betha had been cut by that demon. She'd whispered that something was wrong, and it felt like his heart was going to burst out of his chest. Yet, she had held her own. He had watched her take out a demon while avoiding getting shot with fire. It was a move they had practiced again and again.

He turned toward Parian, who was way too pale. His right wing hung at a wrong angle, and blood dripped down his back.

"Can't you just vanish it?" asked Carter.

"No, never put away a wing while its bleeding or broken. It won't ever heal correctly."

"How do you want me to do this?"

"Cauterize the wound with your angel fire. Once I stop bleeding, I'll be able to tell if I need you to cut it off."

Bile rose in Carter's mouth. He wasn't sure he was going to be able to cut off Parian's wing, even if the older angel told him to. When Parian turned around, though, he had to admit he wasn't sure how it was going to be saved.

"Oh, Parian."

"It's okay. I am alive. I will see my son again. You need to stop the bleeding—my fingers are numb."

Carter raised his blade and pressed the glowing metal against the deep claw marks on the main branch of the wing. Parian muffled a scream, and his body shook. "I am sorry, my friend," said Carter.

Parian turned back around. "I'll be okay."

"Let me take the child."

"No, you need your sword. I can't summon angel fire right now." Parian leaned against the doorway, the child still in his arms. "I just need a moment before I try to move my wing."

"I don't know if I can cut your wing off," whispered Carter.

"You can and you will if it's needed. It will eventually grow back after I get home." Parian pulled the child to his chest and cuddled her. "We will get you somewhere safe, little one." He pulled away from the gargoyle child. "I am just going to set you down for a moment. Then we will get moving again."

Parian set the child down and then tried to move his wing. Carter watched the muscles twitch in his back and the feathers try to move.

"It needs to be removed. It's broken right after the joint." He took a deep breath. "You need to cut it off—not next to my back, but right after that first joint. It will grow back faster that way. I'll keep the other wing. Once you make the cut, apply angel fire. I might pass out. If so, leave me hidden and get out of here."

"We aren't going to leave you behind," said Betha.

Her back was still to them, and her sword was out. "You are coming with us."

The child started to whimper.

"It's okay little one. You will be okay." Parian kneeled on the ground next to the child and hummed a merry tune. Carter flinched at the sound. It was one that Kellion would sing to him and his brother when they were little. One of the only songs that would put them to sleep.

"Do it," said Parian between verses.

Carter raised his sword and straightened Parian's wing out. He gave it his all, and the broken mass tumbled to the ground. His angel fire quickly spread, and the wing turned to ash. Once the wound was cauterized, he stepped back, pulling the fire back inside himself. Parian's body shook, but he remained kneeling. His remaining wing vanished from view with the stump of the other.

"You did well calling it back to yourself," said Parian.

"*There are more incoming,*" whispered Angie. "*I can keep picking them off one by one, but we can't stay here.*"

A shadowed figure flew overhead, then Derrik landed. "What happened?"

Betha responded. "We need to move."

Derrik had been resting when he noticed that Carter had taken off into the sky. At first, he had thought he was just working on his speed, but it had seemed strange.

Then he noticed smoke in the distance. Closer than it

should have been. Derrik had moved as quickly as he could through the sky. The wind had helped him, pushing him faster in that direction, but it had also kept the smoke from blowing toward their camp. Fear gripped him as he flew.

The smoke was coming from a small village close to Rock Camp. It was one where he had stayed before they set up camp on the mountain. How had they missed the smoke? Where were the sentries?

Figures stood in the clearing, and he landed quickly. Dead bodies were everywhere. Gargoyles he had known since he was young were dead. Parian held a small child, clearly too young to be on her own. The angel's wings were not visible, which wasn't good. Parian loved to fly almost as much as Derrik did. For one who was native to the sky to lose it was bad indeed.

"Follow me," Derrik said after the Starwalker urged them to move.

Derrik turned. He knew these woods from when he was a little. He wondered where his mother was. Last he knew, she was here in the village. But there hadn't been anyone fleeing this way, and no one from the village had come up to Rock Camp. He felt a lump of sadness that he put away, with all the grief for his people and the losses in this war. The price they were paying for turning their back on their duty was high, but at least it would not be their extinction. The Starwalker was here, she was helping them, and she was noble. It would all work out, even if he worried his mother, like so many others, wouldn't see it.

Angie kept to the shadows, and as demons crept closer, she yanked them into the shadow plane and killed them. One by one she had reduced the count by at least ten. The demons had been going back to where she assumed the portal was, near where Betha had appeared back on her radar.

She wasn't sure how many more there were, but this was too close to where the demons were trying to go. Even if the portal was closed, they still would rendezvous here. They needed to leave this place and find somewhere that was easier to defend.

"Carter, we need to find somewhere else to regroup. Demons keep going to where Betha closed the portal."

A demon on all fours tried to walk through the shadow she was in. Angie quickly tore out its throat. It seemed like a bear but wrong. Long talons, but at least it moved slowly.

"Derrik knows a place. We are following him."

"Lead the way," responded Angie. *"I will keep picking off any that get too close."*

The group headed north back the way they had come, but much more slowly. Angie kept to the shadows wherever possible, all senses focused on anything moving in their direction. She followed the group deeper into the forest she had run through before. It provided more shadows for her to walk through. Carter skirted the area where they had taken out a group of demons on the way to Betha. Hopefully, they wouldn't run into anything else on the way back to Rock Camp.

"*Why aren't ya'll flying? Have Derrik take Betha,*" Angie asked Carter and Betha.

"*Parian can't fly,*" said Betha. Her voice held barely contained fury.

"*What?*" Angie shouted.

"*He lost a wing,*" sent Carter.

Angie didn't know that was possible. It also explained why the group was moving on foot. The journey back would take over an hour. Concern filled Angie. The demons had attacked a tiny village close by— she slipped back to it in the shadows to make sure no one was following them.

The giant wolf stayed in darkness as she peered out into the village square they had just left. More demons had gathered. They headed toward where the portal had been. This wasn't good.

Smoke filled the air and huts burned. Hopefully it would cover the smell of Betha, Carter, and the others passing through this area. Demons yapped and growled near the portal. They had discovered it was gone.

The group of cat-like demons were joined by the same type of dog creatures from so long ago in the night-club. A tall figure walked out of the underbrush, and Angie froze. It walked upright and had a sword. Tall horns rose from its forehead, and its skin was a deep brown with red stretch marks. Fangs jutted down from its upper jaw.

It spoke in a demanding voice, though Angie had no idea what it said. The various demons dispersed in different directions. She focused only on the ones heading north. Three of the cat-like creatures went in that direction. Angie could handle three.

She faded into the darkness and appeared further into the underbrush. Angie was silent as she stalked the cats. They spread themselves out, which would work out to her benefit. The first, she yanked into the shadows and ripped its throat out. The blood tasted horrible to her, but it was better than letting it go on its way.

She dispatched the next one quickly as well. The third froze and seemed to know something was up. It let out a cry before she could yank it into the darkness.

"Angie, are you okay?" asked Betha.

"I'm fine, just taking care of some cats."

She peered out from the shadows of a large tree, wondering if someone was going to respond to the cry. A tall shadow walked among the trees. Shit.

"Carter, we have an upright behind us. It might not be trailing us. I don't know. It has a sword," sent Angie. She made sure it only went to him. This was not a fight Betha could take on. This demon held himself like one of the Guards from Terra.

It spoke again in that language that she did not understand. It sent a shiver down her spine. The wolf in her wanted to growl a challenge, but she resisted. The element of surprise was important. She needed to take this guy out quickly before he knew what was coming. Unfortunately, he stepped forward into an area of sunlight between two trees.

Angie faded from view and circled back in the direction from which he had come. He needed to move into darker shadows for her to grab him. In the shadow plane, she could take him down easily. When she yanked someone there, they couldn't see or hear anything. They just froze in place. It made her job easier even though it left a bad taste in her mouth.

The demon paused in the bright light and tilted his head to the sky. Angie stared at his back, wondering why it caught her attention. He reached upward, and wings unfolded from his shoulders.

"Shit, he has wings!"

He crouched down to jump skyward, and Angie jumped out of the shadows onto his back. It knocked him to his knees, and she raked her claws down, trying to shred the wings. Her claws caught something because he growled in pain. Then he rolled forward, trying to fling her off. Angie let him. She flew into the bushes, snagged a shadow, and vanished.

The crash in the shadow plane didn't hurt. She quickly peered back out into the clearing. The smell of blood rose from her paws. The demon studied the bushes and glanced every which way. He stayed in the small clearing. Blood dripped down from his wings, and they didn't look like they could be used. Yet, she couldn't be sure.

"I think I shredded his wings," she sent.

Angie checked on the progression of her friends. They had added more distance away from her, which was great. They were so much closer to Rock Camp. Close enough that Derrik could get the two other soldiers that were there for help getting the group back safely.

Part of her wanted to just fade away and catch up with her friends. The demon turned in a circle, eyeing the underbrush intently. If she could stay patient, darkness would be on her side. The sun was moving across the sky. Each breath seemed to take forever.

Five minutes, then she'd be able to see if the shadows hit him. Angie stayed in the shadow realm. She didn't want the smell of her bloodied paws to give her away. A yip sounded much farther south, and the demon turned in that direction. If he let down his guard, she could take him.

He turned again, and his right foot slipped into the shadows. It took everything to not dart at him.

"Let him relax, you have this. Just be patient. Deep breaths. In and out," Angie thought to herself.

Another yip came from the south, and he spun in that direction. She struck. But so did he. Her teeth dug into his calf, and his sword stabbed into her shoulder. Pain radiated downward, but she yanked back. He fell to the ground and pulled his sword back to stab at her again. Angie put all of her weight into yanking him into the darkness.

Once inside, he went still, sword forgotten. Blood dripped down her fur, and she didn't have long before she lost consciousness. The sword strike had been masterful, especially with so little warning. She knew she couldn't have done it. Maybe Carter could have. The demon tried to crawl to his feet, but Angie was there as soon as his throat was in range. Her teeth tore into him, bringing him down. She slipped out of the shadows and almost tumbled to the ground.

"Angie!" Betha yelled as soon as she was out of the shadow realm.

"Coming!"

Her shoulder was a mess, but she didn't dare shift away the damage. She wasn't sure if she would have the strength to shift back to wolf. Yet, the blood would make an easy trail to follow. Instead, she eyed the dark shadows in the distance and moved through them. It was slower than she would like, peeking out enough to teleport to the next area of darkness. Her paw stopped taking weight, and she realized she was getting lightheaded.

"*I got this,*" she said to herself.

"*I'm coming, Angie. Hold on,*" said Carter. Angie could feel him getting closer. This time, she stumbled out of the shadows.

He flew overhead. "*You need to shift now!*"

Angie reached toward her human form, then fell into a different kind of darkness, the kind that came with unconsciousness.

THIRTEEN

Betha watched as more and more gargoyles landed in the clearing near the rock edge of Rock Camp. It seemed each arriving group was bigger than the last. All appeared shell-shocked, some badly wounded, and others jumped at each little movement. The children were the most shaken up. Anyone who could fly had been loaded up with small children, who couldn't fly long distances, and sent to fly north as fast as they could. Others had stayed behind to give them time.

It was devastating.

Talli had shown up covered in blood, a spear clenched in one hand. She had given orders and directed group after group to retreat to Mountain Hold. As soon as the fliers caught their breath and had a bite to eat, they were ordered on. They didn't have enough tents or sleeping spaces for everyone. The clearing on the edge of the mountain was protected, but small. Mountain Hold was bigger and safer.

"I failed them," whispered Talli. Her eyes tracked a

group with five children among them heading north over the mountain. "I should have ordered all the children north when Samson said we should. I failed."

Betha approached. "We didn't think closing portals would create this type of response. All we can do is learn from this."

"Whole villages were wiped out. We thought they were safe."

"You couldn't know how many tears there were, and I didn't think to try to explain," said Betha.

Carter and Derrik had brought an unconscious Angie back. She had been out cold, and Carter had let Betha know her friend had lost a lot of blood. They had taken her to the tent they had been sleeping in.

"How does it look now?" asked Talli.

"Maybe two more days to close the rest of the tears. The more I close, the faster they heal. That's not including the portals. The one to the angels' realm is far to the south, and one of the ones to the hells is near it. Plus the other one to the hells thats about halfway between here and there."

"That southern portal was where the bulk of the battle has been before now. A few of the villages in the southern plains had been attacked, but nothing this far north."

Two gargoyles approached and bowed their heads at Talli. "What news do you want to spread?" one asked.

"All noncombatants are to retreat to Mountain Hold," she replied. "Any injured, any children, anyone who can't hold a spear or sword. Sing it as far and wide as you can.

Leave everything behind, flee to Mountain Hold. They will take any clan."

"What about those who have lost the sky?"

The question confused Betha, and she waited to hear Talli's response.

"They will be welcome, wings or no wings. We will get them up to the hold even if we need to create slings. Our people are what matters!"

They nodded at her words and then headed south. The two flew faster than anyone Betha had ever seen.

"They will spread the word as quickly as possible. Even to settlements not attacked."

Talli stared toward the south, over the treetops. Smoke still rose in the distance near the village where Betha had rescued Parian.

"What will you do now?" asked Betha.

"I have to go north," uttered the elder. "One of us has to survive, and I know the other Elders are down south. Sir Samson as well. I can't leave our people without a leader."

"It is the right thing to do."

"What's going on?" asked Carter. He appeared from the cluster of tents. Betha quickly filled him in, and he nodded.

"Angie fought an upright demon. She took him out, but that doesn't mean more won't come," said Carter.

"How long do you think this area will be safe?" asked Betha.

"No idea. We need to act as if it isn't already," replied Carter.

"Nowhere is safe but Mountain Hold," answered Talli

in English. Her response surprised Betha. "I know some of your tongue. Not much." Talli winked. "There isn't a portal to Mountain Hold. It is our only city. Made of white stone, high in the mountains."

Betha hoped that those flying to the city made it there safely. This had to end. "I should go back in-between tonight."

Carter's head snapped back in her direction. "I don't think that's safe."

"The in-between is the safest place for me."

"We will wait until Angie is up."

"Carter—"

"No, you already closed a bunch of tears and went back in for more. Then you fought a group of demons, protecting a child. You need to rest." Frustration poured through the bond.

"I didn't mean to upset you," said Betha. She resisted the urge to kick a small stone near her feet off the cliff.

"You need to take care of yourself. If something happens to you, any chance of stopping the demons in this world, or any other, disappears."

Carter's words washed over her, and she knew he was right. It was hard looking at these people and seeing them suffer. Yet, how much more did she have in her tonight? She still hadn't eaten. Had she even had something to drink? She couldn't remember.

"Eat, get something to drink, and take a nap. It will help." Carter motioned her toward the tents and the nearby campfire.

"What about you?"

He smirked. "I'll be doing the same. You keep me on my toes."

They approached the fire, and Derrik handed over a bowl of stew. "You must eat, Starwalker." His hands were shaking.

"Are you okay, Derrik?" asked Betha.

He stared at her shook his head. "You are more of a fighter than I am. I could have been a fighter—I was skilled when I was young, but I walked away from that. Now that I passed the trials, I must not. That village was where my mother was. I could do nothing even if I had been there."

Pain rolled across her. Parian had said the only survivor was the child. Betha set the bowl of stew down and hugged Derrik. "I'm so sorry." She figured out a way to wrap her arms around him while not hitting his wings. His wings sagged in the air, and Betha pulled away. "She might have made it out. Keep faith."

Derrik shook his head. "We have to get to that portal to the hells. I need to do my part to save my people."

"We will. Tonight, we need to eat and stay strong. But we will get there, Derrik." They would find a way to get him close to that portal. They would stop this. Somehow.

BEFORE SUNRISE THE NEXT MORNING, the three of them were up. Betha had tried to argue that Angie should rest more, but no one listened. Instead, Angie had eaten everything she could get her hands on and drank a bunch of water.

The goal was to close as many tears as she could today.

Derrik set her down in the clearing near the portal and gave her an extra tight hug. Carter gave her a questioning look, but she shook her head not to comment. Angie set off in her wolf form after Betha made sure she didn't have any wounds left. It didn't matter that Angie said that wasn't how it worked. Her wounds healed when she shifted, but blood loss couldn't be shifted away. The tall trees surrounding the clearing didn't feel as safe as they had before.

"Remember to pace yourself," said Carter.

"I know," said Betha. "I will be careful. You guys as well. I am safe and sound in there. There won't be any peeking today, only moving from one to the next."

Derrik jumped upward toward the sky. He had been quiet since the night before, which she understood. Yet right now, there wasn't any way to get him close enough to the portal to the hells for him to bond with it. Talli had forbidden him from fighting before she had left and it seemed he was instead going quiet. Betha wondered if she could bring him through the in-between. It was something to try, eventually. If they couldn't think of another way. Her concern was that it might kill him.

"I'll see you guys soon," she sent to the two most important people in her world.

Carter gave her a grin before joining Derrik in the sky. Angie's eyes peered out from the underbrush. Two glowing orbs. Seeing them made her feel better about walking into the portal.

"You got this. Let's wrap this up and go home," her friend sent.

Betha nodded and darted into the portal. It was the first time Angie had mentioned home. Were they really going to head out as soon as the portals were taken care of? Was that the plan?

"You seem preoccupied," whispered Magson.

Betha stopped her circling thoughts. "A little. Yesterday was a bad day in the war."

"Good luck, Starwalker."

His voice faded away, and the fireflies arrived in force, lighting up the darkness surrounding her.

"All right guys, we need to get these tears closed." It went quicker than she thought it would. All of them seemed to be natural tears—no more were created with a knife. That gave her hope that there wasn't another knife out there in this world.

The next tear was actively being used, but Betha didn't pause or peek. All that mattered was that she closed it. If no more demons could sneak back and forth, it would help so much. No more back doors. No more surprised villages.

"Where is the next one?"

Her head ached a bit and she was a little sweaty, but overall Betha felt fine. Either she was getting better at using her gifts or the world was getting easier to heal with the more tears that were closed. Maybe both. She had no idea, nor anyone to ask to be certain.

The fireflies danced in the same spot.

"Was that it?"

She knew she had moved quickly and had closed at

least twenty tears. Some big, some small, but one right after another. Yet, it didn't seem like that was enough when she thought of the map in her mind.

"So, back to Magson then."

She turned back the way she had come, but the fireflies dove at her face. They pointed her in a different direction. "Okay, we can go that way."

Betha followed them and was surprised she had only taken a few steps when the light blue portal came into view. Shortcuts were nice, especially when she was done for the day.

"I think we did it, Magson."

He didn't respond to her comment. The hair on the back of her neck rose, and she lightly touched the portal. She peered out, and everything looked okay. Betha pushed through into the clearing. A twang sounded, and something bit at her neck. She reached up and was shocked to find a dart. Like from the movies on Terra. A tranquilizer dart, or something.

The world went from being normal to turning too bright. Someone grunted something and then a pair of hands tried to yank her out of the portal.

"Betha, come back. I can protect you. Backward Starwalker, please!"

But the person pulling on her arm tugged harder, and she stumbled farther away from the portal.

Then everything went dark.

FOURTEEN

Betha could feel her body being tossed around, but she couldn't force her eyes open. She tried to reach out to Angie and Carter, but her mind was fuzzy. They were nearby, but Betha couldn't ask them anything, only sense their presence. As she reached out with her power, she realized they were near a portal and moving closer. It glowed red in her mind.

Panic filled her, and she tried again to open her eyelids, but she couldn't control her body at all. The portal loomed closer. Sounds in another language surrounded her, and she couldn't move. Angie and Carter were nearby, then Angie vanished from her senses, and Carter quickly followed. They had to have gone through the portal.

Time stopped.

Everything went quiet, and she could feel something near her face. Whatever it was poked at her mind, questioning her state. This had to be the in-between. Maybe it could stop her from going through the portal. But then she would be leaving Angie and Carter behind.

Betha couldn't do it. She couldn't speak, but she pushed her feelings out toward the in-between. This had to happen, she needed to follow her anchors. She was going to make all of this right. Somehow it would all work out.

Everything unfroze. Yelling erupted as she was brought to the other side of the portal. She was shifted in someone's arms and then she could understand what was being said, like a switch was flipped inside her mind. Betha felt like she did with the gargoyles and their language, when she had suddenly understood.

"Take her to the prison with the other two. The princess is on her way."

Betha could feel Angie and Carter again, though they were farther away from her than she would have thought. Given how far away they were from her location, it must have taken her plenty of time to come through the portal.

Whoever was carrying her moved quickly. The feeling in her fingers started to come back as they headed down some stairs. It wasn't as bad as the poison from the Piccum demons since it was reversing so quickly, and she was thankful for that small mercy. Betha forced herself to stay relaxed. The more they underestimated her, the better. She heard a gate creak open, then she was placed on something hard. Hands groped along her body, and she felt her sword removed from its scabbard. Yet, that was all they took before leaving.

Betha wiggled her toes in her boots. They hadn't

found the knife or the feather. The feeling was coming back throughout her body, and she hoped it would happen quicker. Faster. She needed to figure out where they were.

Pain washed over her, and her body jerked out of her control.

"That should wake her up," said a female voice with a note of cruelty.

Betha's eyes snapped open. Everything hurt. Whatever they'd just done to her, she could feel all of her bones, and now they ached. It was horrible.

"Aww, didn't you like the electricity? That sucks for you."

Something stabbed into her side again, and she tried to roll away. A stone wall stopped her from putting any real distance between it and her, but at least the shock ceased.

It hurt. Panic washed over her, and she focused on her breathing. The electricity didn't come again, and she opened her eyes to slits to peek over her shoulder. At least she could move. The ceiling was rough stone, and Betha quickly sat up. Everything spun, but she saw that she was in a cell with a female demon next to the door made of metal bars.

"Finally, the Traveler the king has demanded," said a voice that dripped with seductive honey.

Betha blinked and could make out the form in more detail. She was tall with long red hair, and her eyes were a deep blue. A black crown was on her head, glowing faintly red in the light. The demon woman wore black polished armor and had a wicked-looking sword at her side. In her hand was a piece of crystal, and Betha had a feeling it was somehow the source of electricity that had been causing her pain. Given the demon woman's crown, she assumed this was someone related to the prince.

"I don't know what the fuss is about. Only that he wants you, little Traveler," the demon, who must be the princess, continued.

Three walls of the cell were made up of the metal bars, and the cells on either side were occupied. The one on her left had Carter in it. He was on a stone bed, not moving. On her other side, Angie was chained to the wall, naked. Her eyes glowed in the light. A metal collar encircled her neck.

Betha moved toward the bars closest to Angie but stayed near the bed she was on. Her eyes remained on the princess. Betha did not want to get closer to her since she had the crystal. This was not a situation she was prepared for. At all.

"*Angie,*" said Betha.

"*Relax. I am here, just a little tied up,*" Angie replied. It was true—she didn't look beaten up or anything. Just naked and chained. Her feet touched the floor, barley. Betha had no idea how she was so calm.

"Stay right where you are, Traveler," said the princess. "If you do anything, I will hurt them. The king hasn't demanded them, you see. Though having my own private angel is fascinating. Not to mention my own lapdog." The demoness laughed. "You have provided entertainment for years to come."

Betha froze again as the demon motioned with the

crystal. Betha wasn't sure if she needed to be touched or if it could send electricity through her from afar.

"*She pressed it to your side before,*" said Angie.

"Who are you?" asked Betha.

"The whelp speaks our language! How quaint." The woman moved farther into the room. "I am the Princess of Hell. Ruler of the Second and Third Circles." A grin covered her face, revealing sharply pointed teeth.

"What do you want?" asked Betha.

"You are slow. I already said, my king demanded I bring you here. So here you are." The princess motioned to the cell they were in. "You are a guest of ours, and once the king is here, you are his."

Betha did not want to meet the king of hell, especially not after closing most of the pathways into Sky World. Panic rolled through her, and she dug her fingers into her palms. Maybe she should have stayed in the in-between and not joined her Anchors. But Betha would not leave her anchors behind.

"But what do you want?" she finally asked again.

The princess shrugged. "Orders are orders, even to one such as I. I had to bring you here no matter what. Mission accomplished. Now I am free to do as I wish."

"And what is that?" asked Betha. In the movies, keeping the villain talking was important. She could ask questions. Maybe she would find out why the demons were doing what they were doing.

"Why would I tell you? I just wanted to see what all of the trouble was about. Plus, I am waiting for a guest. Without their help, I wouldn't have gotten you, let alone all three of you. I need to keep my promises, after all."

"Keep her talking," whispered Carter in her head. *"It will give us time to fight off whatever drugs they hit us with."*

"But I do have a question for you. My scouts discovered a portal they could not go through to Sky World. How was that done?" asked the princess.

Betha realized she was asking about the portal that Magson had bonded to. "Why do you care?"

"Curiosity. Can it be done anywhere? Does it only block demons?" The princess crept closer to Betha. The crystal was still in her hand. Betha flinched. "If you let me know, I might even let one of your friends go." Red eyes stared down at her.

Betha scooted backward on the bed. She had no idea how that information could be used. Or how it would help the princess or the demons. The princess moved closer, and Betha tried to let herself relax. Pain was pain—she could do this. She'd survived it twice already. She would survive it again.

"Do you promise to let them both go if I tell you?" asked Betha. Didn't demons make deals in the history books? This could work.

The princess froze, eyes narrowed. "I will let one of them go. My choice."

"You have to let Angie go—alive—through the portal," answered Betha. "Do you promise?"

The princess tossed the crystal from one hand to the other. It seemed like she really wanted the information. She moved closer to Betha, leaning over the bed, and staring down at her. The bright red eyes flickered blue reminding her of Carter, but they held a malice so severe it was almost a physical force, far more malice than she had ever seen before. Even with the prince.

"*Betha, what are you doing?*" asked Angie. "*What are you saying?*"

Someone whispered from the doorway near the stairs, breaking the tension. "Princess, the slaves are causing some issues above. Can you please provide some support?"

Bright red light spilled from her crown, and the princess slammed her fist into the wall above Betha. Dust rained down on her. "Fine. I'll deal with the slaves. Give the keys to the human when she gets here."

The princess swept out of the cell and slammed the metal door behind her. It locked shut. The guard followed the princess out, leaving the hallway empty.

BETHA SHOOK HER HEAD, shocked that they were gone. It took a minute to relax her fingers enough to flex them. She could do this. They would find a way out.

"*Shit, what now?*" asked Angie. "*I can't shift with this collar on. Can you move yet, Carter?*"

"*Not yet,*" said Carter. "*I can feel my body coming back, but it's taking its time.*"

Betha jumped to her feet, stumbling as she moved toward the door of her cell. She shook. "*We need to get out of here.*" Neither one of her Anchors responded immediately, and she turned toward Angie, then glanced at Carter. "*We will get out of here. Right?*"

"*Can you use the knife?*" asked Carter.

Betha patted her boot to reassure herself that the knife was still hidden there. It was. *"I have no idea how,"* answered Betha, *"but I can try."* The knife had been used to create tears between two worlds. Yet, Kyra had mentioned a Traveler had created it. Up until now, her focus had been on keeping it safe while she figured out what to do with it. Kyra wanted it destroyed, but during Betha's dreaming visits to the starry place, it seemed she shouldn't destroy it. Hopefully, she could use it to get them all out of this world.

A door slammed somewhere in the distance, and she jumped, yanking her fingers away from her boot. Heavy footsteps came down the stairs toward them. Betha moved to the center of the cage. She did not want to be on the bed whenever this person came in, not after she had gotten caught between the wall and the princess last time. The center of the room had more area to move in.

One of the demon guards entered the hallway. He had a bored expression on his face. Small horns protruded from his forehead, and his skin was completely black. He wore leather pants and a cloth shirt, but no armor, though he had a sword at his side. A cloaked figure entered behind the demon. The heavy brown cloak covered their features, but the princess had mentioned they were human. What was a human doing working with the demons?

The figure turned toward the demon and held out a hand. "Keys?" The voice was female, which surprised Betha, and very demanding.

The demon handed them over, rolling his eyes.

"Leave us!" commanded the woman.

The guard quickly headed back toward the stairs. "Don't let any of them out or she will have your head!" the demon tossed over his shoulder.

The figure waited until the guard was gone, then stood in front of the door to Betha's cell. "Some Travelers are close to their Anchors. I wonder how close you are to these two..." Her voice trailed off as she stared into her cell. Betha tried to see beneath the hood, but the woman stepped back. "Some see their Anchors as their family, others toss them away at the first chance. I wonder which you are?"

"What do you want?" asked Betha. But that wasn't the real question she had. She wanted to know why a human was working with the demons.

"Where is the knife?"

Betha quickly replied, "I destroyed it." This was about the knife? Why did a human want the knife?

"Liar. Kyra thinks you destroyed it, but I know better. You wouldn't have destroyed it." She slowly paced outside the three cells. First in front of Angie's cell, then she barely shook her head before moving outside of Carter's. She unlocked the door and slipped the keys inside her cloak. Betha wasn't sure why she was keeping her face covered.

"*Carter, can you move?*" asked Betha.

"*Not yet.*"

"Betha, I heard a rumor that you have a crush on your Anchor," whispered the woman. She slowly moved deeper into Carter's cell. "I wonder how much you care about him or that wolf over there? What will you do for them?" She ran her fingers up his arm.

Betha didn't know how to respond. Her thoughts stopped. No one knew, or at least Betha thought no one knew but Angie.

The figure pulled a knife out and ran it up his arm. It nicked him in one spot.

"What are you doing?" asked Betha.

"Whatever is necessary. Where is the knife?" responded the cloaked figure.

"Gone!"

She stabbed the knife into Carter's shoulder. It was right where the demon had stabbed him when he had almost died. Carter cried out. Her mind flashed back to the clearing and how she had anchored him. Betha could feel pain rolling down the bond, and then it was shut off.

"Stop!" Betha's voice echoed down the hallway.

The woman left the knife in Carter's shoulder and moved closer to the bars of Betha's cell. "Next time I touch the knife, it will be to slice his throat. Tick tock, little Traveler. I don't like playing games anymore."

Betha didn't know what to do. She couldn't watch Carter die in front of her. Yet, the knife was dangerous, and it might be the only way for them to get out of this situation. How did this person know about the knife? And what Kyra thought?

"*Don't give it to her,*" croaked Carter in the bond.

"*Distract her, Betha. Get her into your cell,*" added Angie. "*Away from the knife and Carter.*"

The person turned back toward Carter, and her fingers moved to the knife still in his shoulder.

"Stop! I have it. It's hidden on me," said Betha.

The person turned toward her, and Betha caught a

glimpse of red lips twisted in a cruel smile. The cloaked figure quickly exited Carter's cell and fumbled with the keys, then unlocked the door to her cell. Betha kept her eyes off of the open door and on the hooded figure. As far as she knew, the woman didn't have another weapon.

"Get the knife quickly, before the princess gets back, little Traveler," said the hooded woman. They were close enough for Betha to see under the hood, but she didn't recognize the woman. She was older, and definitely human, but not someone Betha knew.

Betha leaned down toward her boot, moving as slowly as she could. "Why do you want it?"

"It will let someone go anywhere, if they have enough power. I thought Kyra would be the one to bring it to Terra, but I was wrong. The demons had it instead. Who would have thought they would bring it to Terra? Give it to me. We can't let them get near it again."

"*I know that voice,*" said Carter. "*Get her close to the bars between our cages.*"

Betha undid the hidden opening to the sheath and pulled out the knife. The woman darted forward to grab it, but Betha elbowed her in the face. It knocked her back for a second before she dove to grab at the knife again. Betha's hand shook—she didn't want to stab her.

"You will give it to me!" the woman screeched. She scratched at Betha's arm, trying to get the handle. Betha shoved her as hard as she could at the bars. Somehow, Carter was suddenly standing on the other side. He grabbed her hood, yanking her close to him. He pulled the knife out of his shoulder and stabbed her in the same spot where she stabbed him.

"Andrea!" His voice was harsh as he named her. "You betrayed the council!"

Andrea cried out in pain. She struggled against the bars, but he held on to her cloak. "That pathetic council who listened to every word I said? All that matters is getting back home, and I *will* get that knife!"

"*Betha, use the knife! Flee,*" said Angie. "*You need to go now! I hear someone coming!*"

Carter held Andrea back as she struggled to get away from him.

"We can go together," said Betha.

"I can hear them coming, Betha. Go!" demanded Angie.

Betha pulled the knife free and fumbled with it. It sliced into her hand, and she almost dropped it.

"I don't know how to use it!" she exclaimed.

"Just do it! You are a freaking Traveler! You walk among the stars." Angie's voice was frantic. Her chains rattled.

"No!" Andrea broke the cloak's clasp, slipping free of Carter, who crashed to the floor. She tried to tackle Betha, but Betha focused on the in-between, the darkness, and the fireflies. Light flashed through the room, and both Andrea and Betha vanished.

FIFTEEN

Something flew at Angie, and she caught it by reflex. It was the keys. She focused on getting the damn collar off. She could hear footsteps by the doorway that led to the stairs. They did not have time. Suddenly, the lock released, and she slid the collar off. She dashed to her cell door. It wasn't even locked. Carter was her priority. He was still bleeding from his shoulder. She stuffed the keys in his pocket just in case. Andrea's cloak was still in his hands. The keys must have been inside.

"Come on, we need to go," she said to him.

"Leave me," answered Carter. He looked pale, and he breathed shallowly.

"None of that nonsense. Put pressure on it."

Angie slid an arm under his shoulder and led him down the hall. Although he was taller and broader than she was, no shifter was weak, and Angie was stronger than most shifters. She'd carry him if she had to. They needed to find a different set of stairs up. More cells lined the hall, but they offered no protection. The open door at the end was unlocked, thankfully. She stumbled through with Carter and found more steps. They had to keep going.

The stairs were hard, and shouting came from below. A hallway branched off the first landing, but she kept going up. The building seemed to be less maintained the further up she went. Some of the steps were cracked. At the second landing, there was another door, this one broken, hanging open, leading to another hallway. This hallway was empty, and she headed down it. Distance would be good. She peeked in each empty room they passed until she found one with a window. The floor was covered in dust, but it didn't matter if they followed their footprints.

"Perfect. We got this, Carter."

He mumbled something in reply, but she didn't understand. He would be okay. Betha was safe, now it was up to her to get them out. She set him down near the window. Angie shut and locked the door behind them and shifted. One moment she was human, the next a giant wolf. She peeked out of the window and saw exactly what she was looking for—shadows next to a rundown building in the distance. It was farther than she liked, but they needed that distance.

"Carter, don't panic. Stay still. Take a deep breath," she sent him through their link.

"What are you doing?" he mumbled, clearly fading.

"Do it. Now!" He took a deep breath and then Angie yanked him into the shadow plane. Just because she hadn't done it before didn't mean she couldn't. It had to be possible. Then she yanked him out next to the

building. The wolf took a deep breath as Carter sputtered.

"*Shhh,*" said Angie. "*Not safe yet.*" He was still breathing, that was what mattered.

She spotted another deep shadow farther down the roadway where the buildings looked even more worn. Hopefully, it would be somewhere they could hide.

"*Another deep breath. Ready?*"

"*No!*"

"*Now!*"

Carter responded to the command in her mental voice, and again she pulled him through. When she pulled him out, he gulped air. "I need a moment. Please," he whispered.

A gasp behind them had Angie turning, her teeth bared in a silent growl. A small troll with curved horns was carrying a basket. They were her height, which was strange. They looked from Carter, who was bleeding, back to her. Carter waved at them and said something in the troll's language. The troll responded. They motioned to the doorway they had come out of.

"*What are they saying?*" asked Angie.

"They will help us."

"*Why?*"

"Slaves stick together."

THE TROLL HELPED Carter through the doorway, then shut the door behind them and directed them down a narrow hallway. Doorways lined it, but there were no doors.

More trolls peered out at them from crowded rooms as they passed by. Low murmurs of voices stopped and started as they passed. Everything was dim and dusty. The people looked beaten down. His shoulder hurt.

The troll led them into a much bigger room toward the end of the hall. Angie padded down the hallway, still in her shifted form. He kept a hand on her back, and it helped steady him. The blood pouring out of the wound had slowed. He was doing better but was still slightly dizzy.

The room they entered opened up, and a fire was going in a crumbling fireplace. Thick carpets lined the floors. Trolls were laid out all over the place, and many had bandages covering wounds. A skinny figure looked up, and Angie froze beside him.

"She's an elf," said Angie.

The elf approached them quickly. "Oh, my fates, you're a shifter," whispered the elf. "How did you get here? He's bleeding." She turned toward the troll and spoke rapidly in the troll's language. "What happened to him?"

"What always happens," answered the troll. "I need to go get the elder."

Angie whined from under Carter's hand.

The elf turned back to Carter. She looked worn out. Her light brown hair was cut in ragged chunks, and she had dried blood on her clothing. "I can heal some of the damage," she said in a tired voice.

"How are you here?" asked Carter.

"I was taken prisoner when they attacked Red Kill back during the Terra invasion. I can heal, so I am still alive." She approached Carter but froze when Angie growled. Her hands shook. "Uh, I don't mean any harm to your friend. I want to look at his shoulder," she said to the large wolf. Angie sniffed at the floor, and Carter felt her concern. She moved toward the doorway, staying just out of sight of the hallway.

"*I'll keep watch. Get your shoulder fixed,*" ordered Angie.

"She knows you don't mean any harm. She's just on edge," Carter said to the elf.

"I don't blame her. This place is rough. Is your shoulder healing at all?" She had a bruise on one arm in the shape of a large hand.

"Yes, it's healing somewhat, but we just need more time. It was a knife," answered Carter.

The healer nodded and placed her hands on his shoulder. Warmth and light rose from her palms. "I can close it up and give it a jump start, but I don't dare do more than that. I have too many patients today because of the rally last night. Gale says you are on the run from the demons." She froze and pushed against the wound. The heat returned. "You are lucky you aren't dead. That knife had something on it. I don't know what."

Carter shrugged, then wished he hadn't. "We were nabbed on Sky World by the princess's people. Our friend escaped, and now we are trying to as well."

The elf gave him a small smile. "You need to get out before they brand you." She pulled down her ratty shirt, revealing a dark brand on her shoulder. It looked like an old burn. "They can track you. You are lucky the princess didn't do it already. She must not nab slaves very often."

The troll returned and frantically started speaking to the healer, but Carter couldn't follow her words.

"She says there are demons looking for you, and it might be a lieutenant. We can keep you here for a short while, but you will need to keep moving. No one here will say anything, but we can't risk their wrath if they find you here. They might kill all of us just for talking to you. How did your friend escape?"

"She is a Traveler," responded Carter before he could censor himself. The pain in his shoulder had substantially reduced. Even so, he felt like he was floating a little. His angelic healing was having a tough time with whatever poison Andrea had used. The longer they could stay here, the better. Once he was up and moving, his healing would slow down.

"You're anchored?" asked the healer incredulously, running her hands through her very short hair.

Carter blushed. He couldn't help it. When Eric healed him, it was never like this. It almost felt like he was high.

"You guys were the ones who closed the portals on Terra," said the elf. "And you stopped the prince!"

"*She is well informed,*" said Angie. "*Carter, you good?*"

"*Getting there. Can I have ten more minutes?*" His mind was still floaty, and he did not like it one bit. It was hard to focus on things, but the center of his gaze was clearing up.

"What happened to you?" Carter asked the elf.

"Well, the prince captured me. When he was dispatched, I was taken here, and my brand went to the king. He needed a healer, and I guess I was a rare find." Her voice went flat, and her eyes seemed to dim. The dark circles under her eyes stood out. She shook her head. "You have an actual chance of getting out of here. You can let people know where we are."

"My priority is to ensure we aren't used against our Traveler. But I will do what I can," replied Carter.

The troll started frantically speaking after peeking out of the doorway. All Carter caught was something about an elder.

A much older troll walked into the room. He had a staff and thick dark horns, one of which was broken off. His chest was covered with necklaces of sharp teeth, each as long as his pinky. The elder nodded to the healer, and Carter focused on the newcomer. He could feel that he was doing better, but he really needed some water. Carter tried to stand, and Angie dashed closer.

"Be careful. We need you to heal faster," said Angie. She was right. He had no idea how they were going to get out of here, but it was going to take time.

Carter held up a hand to Angie and spoke to the troll. "Elder, we thank you for your presence." His voice croaked a bit. He wondered if his pronunciation was correct. He only knew the basics of the language, and this was a different dialect than he was used to. Following it was hard.

"You are companions of the Starwalker." He paused, staring at them both before nodding again. He reached for his necklaces. " We heard she had been captured. I ask that you give this to the Starwalker to give to the trolls on Terra. We heard stories from the healer that they are free. We will someday be free as well. Soon." The troll took off one of the necklaces with the teeth and crouched down to hand it over to Carter.

"I will do that." Carter carefully took it and slid it over his head. Thankfully, his shoulder was doing better, or that would have hurt.

The elder smiled, showing broken teeth. "Follow. We will take you somewhere hidden. You will be able to get to the portal once you are healed."

"*We need to move. The demons are getting closer. They are going to lead us to a different building, closer to the portal,*" relayed Carter to Angie.

"*Wait, are you okay?*"

"*I can feel it healing,*" answered Carter.

The elder said something to the healer that Carter couldn't make out. The healer shook her head.

"He wants me to finish healing you. He said any troll would agree," said the elf. She moved in and placed her hand back on him. It glowed for several moments, then faded. "Let your people know that some from Terra were taken. Maybe you can find a way to get me out of here." She swayed before sitting on the floor, tears in her eyes. "Tell them Ayda Caffrey from Red Kill is still alive. Let my parents know I might come home someday."

"I will. We will find a way to get you some help," said Carter. He climbed to his feet and was steady. His head felt clearer, and he finally had faith they would get out of there. The elder led them out of the room and down the hallway then out a door. The old troll moved quickly for someone his age. More trolls gathered around them, shifting in place and directing them down alleyways.

Whenever Carter saw a demon, they were rushed out

of sight, or different groups of trolls made a racket. Somehow, they were making it around the outside of the village.

"*Why are they helping us?*" asked Angie.

"*I am going to get this necklace to Garruk, the troll council member,*" answered Carter.

"*But why?*"

"*This was the troll world once. Magnestrial.*"

"*But...where are the giant trees and oceans? Or the great plains they hunted on?*"

Carter understood her questions. Back on Terra, everyone was taught the trolls had to flee their home world. A group settled on Terra, and they were the only survivors. But apparently some other trolls survived here, and the demons took over. Yet, none of the trolls on Terra had ever implied that their people remained slaves. From what he'd heard from Garruk, the trolls on Terra believed all of their kin were dead.

"There is probably not much of that left. As I understand it, this became the Fourth Circle of hell, and it's been ruled by the demon king for centuries."

SIXTEEN

This was one of the reasons the princess hated the Fourth Circle. It seemed they were having never-ending problems with the slaves. By default, since the king was on the Seventh Circle and she ranked higher than his lieutenants, any issues that cropped up fell to her. She couldn't wait to leave.

Akeldama took a deep breath. She just needed a few more days for her plans for the Sixth Circle to bear fruit. If only she could figure out a way to get the king stuck in the Seventh Circle. He was spending more and more of his time there, trying to wrestle the world away from the gargoyles. They hadn't expected the angels to get involved, and it had slowed down their conquest.

Not that she cared. This constant need of the king's to expand had shifted from brilliant to crazy. The more land he controlled, the more erratic he became. When he had given the prince and Akeldama their own lands, things had been calm for several centuries. Then, he'd been driven to expand again, and she couldn't understand it, not really. What land they had was good enough, their people needed help. The demonic population was the lowest in centuries.

The Traveler had also messed with their plans. Tears that they had been using for years to move demons onto the world were suddenly gone. Their troops were stranded in various locations without any way back. Yet, the king kept pushing forward no matter what.

Akeldama would give the Fourth Circle up if she were allowed to, especially given the problems from the trolls. But it wasn't her choice.

Her eyes roamed over the slaves bound in ropes. Each troll was on their knees with a demon standing next to them, and a crowd had formed. Demons with swords and spears kept them at bay.

Yet another uprising. They had increased in frequency and ferocity ever since the king had decided to go after the gargoyle world. It didn't help that he had relocated so many trolls right next to a portal that represented freedom to them. Most did not realize that the other side of the portal wasn't free—demon armies controlled the settlement. It was the first location that they had conquered. So even if a slave somehow made it through the portal, they wouldn't get far.

Akeldama studied the crowd as she approached and wondered about the best way to solve this problem. Killing them would stir up more resentment, but if she had a way to win the slaves over, that could be useful.

"This is your lucky day," her voice rang out over the crowd, and she pushed power to her crown. Each branded slave in the crowd would feel her rank. "The king is on the Seventh Circle of hell, and I am here in his stead." She infused her words with sympathy. "These trolls before you broke the law, and we all know what the king's order would be."

Murmuring broke out in the crowd. She pushed out more emotion through the brands. "Which of these trolls should I grant clemency?" More noise came from the crowd, and she let a small smile form. They were thinking about it. The princess moved to the first troll in line, and the demon next to him backed up.

"Stand up, slave," she ordered softly to the first kneeing troll. The command was sent through the bond, but she could feel him fighting it. His head came up first, and he met her eyes. Bright green orbs stared at her. Then he spit at her.

Anger pounded through every bone in her body, and she resisted bringing her sword up. Power rolled through her, but she contained it. "You have spirit." A flash of pain washed up from her arm, and the princess froze.

Typhon was by her side in an instant. "Princess?" he asked, concerned.

"Find the seer, now!"

He disappeared, teleporting away.

The binding that she had with the seer had broken. There was no way the seer was dead—they needed each other. The break gave the crowd too long to think. A rock sailed through the crowd, but it fell short of hitting her. Eyes filled with hatred watched from the crowd, and someone else threw a piece of pottery.

"Fine, kill them all," ordered the princess. Eight heads rolled across the dusty ground, and the crowd fought with the guards, angered by the sudden, total violence. "Time for everyone to go home! Anyone who disobeys will face the same consequences."

The order lightly rolled over the crowd, and those who were scared caved first. Once some trolls broke away from the crowd, it was easier for others to justify leaving as well. Only a few attacked the demons. Akeldama rolled her eyes as the demons cut down those resisting. The slaves should know better by now.

The dead trolls were a wasted resource. Her father should be here concentrating on bringing back order, not bringing another world into the fold. Such a waste.

Typhon appeared at her side. "Princess, they are gone."

"What?" she growled.

"The Traveler, the seer, and the two you brought with them."

"Send in the scent hounds. We need to find them." Panic and fury rolled over her. The king was on his way from the front line. Yet, the order had been fulfilled. She had brought the Traveler to this forsaken dusty corner of hell. Not her fault his soldiers had lost her and the slaves were rebelling.

Akeldama nodded. She could spin this. Now she needed to find them and create order. "Find any slaves who would enjoy the benefits of being on our side."

"Yes, my princess."

She needed to work quickly.

~

ONE MOMENT, Betha had been in the cell, and Andrea had been running at her. She had focused on the knife, on escape, and then suddenly everything vanished. Betha had a moment where she could feel the darkness and the fireflies before they too vanished. She slammed down on a hard stone surface, and everything hurt. Someone touched her forehead with a cool hand.

"You will be okay dearie, just rest," whispered a kind voice.

Betha let the darkness take her.

WARMTH WASHED OVER HER, and Betha fought her way back to consciousness. Flashbacks of the cell came to her, and she flinched. Automatically, she curled up into a ball. Reaching out, she couldn't feel Angie or Carter. Her mind was empty, yet it wasn't. There was something there, just not her Anchors.

"You are safe here, child." A soft voice spoke from nearby, and Betha tried to get her muscles to relax. She needed to see where she was. Underneath her was a soft blanket. It felt like she was on a bed. Carefully, she peeked out from beneath her arms.

The walls were wooden, and a fire flickered somewhere. A presence was in her mind, and it sent reassuring vibes to her. How was she in a cottage? An actual fairytale cottage. Betha searched for the voice. To her surprise, an older woman sat in a rocking chair next to the bed. Her hair was white and her eyes hazel.

"Ah, there you are. I promise I won't cause you any

harm here. You landed very hard on the stone outside. Is anything broken?" Her voice was calm and soothing. "The grandmother in me wants to check you over, but you are a bit jumpy."

That was what she looked like—someone's grandmother. Thin and clearly fit, but grandmotherly. Betha had no idea how she had gotten here. One moment she had been in the prison cell. Then, the knife. Betha froze and carefully glanced around the cottage. A small table was next to the bed, and the knife sat on it. She forced her eyes back to the grandmother.

"Where am I?" asked Betha.

"You are in my house. But if you are asking about what world you are on, you are not strictly on any world. You are in a node. You should still be with your parents, young one. And you have a knife. It seems you have a story to tell. After that, we need to find your parents."

Betha didn't even know where to start. Part of her wasn't sure that this wasn't something that the demons had cooked up. Another part of her remembered trying to use the knife, and a moment of the in-between before a hard landing.

"Who are you?"

"I am the one guarding this node." The grandmother's eyebrows drew together as she gazed at Betha. Her eyes flicked over to the knife like she was trying to figure out a riddle.

Betha unwound herself and sat up slowly. Her back hurt, but nothing felt broken. This woman hadn't harmed her and instead seemed concerned. Hopefully, it was the truth. "I don't understand what any of that means," whispered Betha.

"Where are your parents?"

"My mother," Betha's voice hitched in her throat, "is dead, and I don't know my father."

The woman made to move forward but paused when Betha flinched. "I am so sorry, dearie. What happened to you?"

Betha stared at her, and the presence in her head pushed the feeling of safety even harder. "My name is Betha, and I am from Terra." She continued with a quick recap. That she had stolen the knife from the demons and was now helping the gargoyle world. She mentioned that she was anchored and only knew one Traveler, Kyra. As she ran through the many trials of the past months, the calm emotions began to run out. Angie and Carter were still with that demon princess, and Carter was injured. As she reached the end of her story, the older woman's eyes opened wide, and her mouth opened. Finally, Betha's words ran out.

"I need to figure out how to get back. My Anchors are in a demon prison," she finished, then fell silent.

"I'm Genessa, Kyra's grandmother. You are Josephine's daughter." The old woman shook her head in disbelief. "Surprise—she wasn't crazy after all."

"Wait, you knew my mother?" Betha's thoughts jolted from worrying about Angie and Carter to her mother.

Genessa climbed to her feet and moved across the room toward the fire. She pulled a kettle off the heat and grabbed some cups. "We need to talk, especially about that knife. You have no idea what you have done."

"None of that matters—my family is being held by demons. I need to get them out." Even so, her mind drifted back to her mother. She wanted answers, but the information wasn't going to fix the life-or-death situation. If it was between the present life of her chosen family or answering questions about the past, her future had to take priority.

Genessa waved a hand. "You have all the time you need. This is a node. Time passes differently here." She motioned to the table. "Relax. Take a seat. Some tea will do you well."

Betha climbed to her feet and grabbed the knife from the bedside table. As soon as her fingers touched it, the presence in her head increased. "What the heck?" Betha poked at it with her mind, and the knife glowed. Light peeked out from under her armor where her mark was.

"That's part of what we need to talk about." Genessa gave her a soft smile as she poured water into the cups. "You have bonded with the Sartovalund. What do you know about the bone knife?"

Betha sat and placed the knife down on the table. Putting it away didn't seem like a nice thing to do, especially with it glowing. The light show vanished. "Only that a Traveler gave their life to create it. It also creates tears between worlds."

A snort from Genessa had Betha glancing up. "It is so much more than that." Genessa poured the hot tea into wooden cups. "The Sartovalund are created by Travelers who are dying. We have several options at that point in our existence, but this one decided that they wanted to help future Travelers. They bound their soul not to a portal or a node, nor even to the leylines themselves where they would be connected to the future, but to their very bones." Genessa set the kettle back down near the fire. "All alone for eternity unless they can find someone worthy. It is a dream, and one that is no longer encouraged. Yet that Traveler finally found that person." She pointed at Betha. "You."

Betha picked the knife back up. "This Traveler was waiting for me?"

Genessa sat next to her. "They were waiting for anyone that the Tree thought was worthy. It isn't just up to the Traveler. Think of it like you are anchored to them. Only the decider is the Tree of Life."

"What does that mean? When I anchored with Angie and Carter, things changed. And what is the Tree of Life?" Betha didn't know which direction to take first—so many questions bubbled up inside her. But she didn't feel like she had time for this conversation, despite what the woman said about time flowing differently. Every moment here was a moment that her family was still captive. And she wasn't sure if she could trust Genessa. Kyra was keeping secrets from her, and she didn't know if Genessa was any different.

"The Tree connects all of the worlds together with the leylines. The leylines are the Tree. Everything is always in a state of change with life."

Despite how thoroughly unhelpful that response was, Betha's thoughts returned to Angie and Carter. "But how did it bring me here, and how do I get back?" Betha picked the knife up again and turned it this way and that.

Genessa didn't answer her question right away. She sipped on the tea in the wooden cup. "I can take you to the portal that will bring you back to the world you came from, but you must promise me that when your Anchors are safe, you will come back." She set her cup down. "There is too much you don't know. Don't use the knife again until then."

"I mean, can't I learn from Kyra?" asked Betha. She glanced down at the knife one last time before sliding it back into her boot under the table.

Genessa smirked, then chuckled. "Kyra is young. Not as young as you, but she has made mistakes. Mistakes that had consequences that are now coming to fruition, it seems, with your talk of demons. If you see her before you return here, tell her that her grandmother says hi."

"You are her grandmother." Betha shook her head. So much of this didn't make sense. It was so much information at once that she couldn't stay on track. "I can come back. I promise. If you tell me how to return."

Genessa held out her hand with her mark. It had faded Anchor marks, so faded that Betha couldn't make them out. Bright and clear, however, she had a tree growing out of the compass rose. Leaves and roots trailed down her arm. Betha touched the mark out of curiosity. Both marks flared and she felt a zap down her arm.

Betha jerked her hand back. "What was that?"

"A promise between Travelers. As I said, you have much to learn. Which is why you need to come back. You will come back when your Anchors are safe." Genessa's gaze went over Betha's shoulder. "A promise is a promise. I will take you to the portal. Come on. It is a quick walk."

She headed out the open doorway that Betha hadn't noticed before. Betha quickly followed and walked out into the moonlight. The full moon was overhead, along with more stars than were possible. A grass path led to a stone circle that looked a lot like the Nexus back on Terra. One doorway was completely dark, bricked up with stones. Her eyes kept going back to it even as she glanced around.

"Do you know what world you were on?" asked the older Traveler.

Betha shrugged. "Not really. I was on the gargoyle world. From there, I went to a different world when I was captured."

Genessa turned toward one of the portals. "Focus on the feeling of going through that portal. The sensation."

Betha stared at her, and Genessa stared back. Finally, Betha closed her eyes and thought back to how she had been yanked through that portal. The questioning in-between, then concern, and then her saying it needed to happen.

"Go, now! Remember you need to come back!"

When Betha opened her eyes, the portal in front of her was glowing red and white. She was doing it.

She was going back. She stepped into the light.

CHAPTER

SEVENTEEN

T he elder troll led Carter and Angie to a different building and up several sets of stairs. Carter was thankful that the healer had worked more on his shoulder. It was strange that this was the first major injury since he had manifested. When he had bonded with Betha, his healing had increased. Now, it was much quicker. He wasn't sure how fast it would have healed on its own though, especially with what the elf healer had said—something had been on that knife. Now he knew he healed much slower from poison. Why did Andrea have poison on her knife? Why did Andrea betray the council? None of it made sense. He still didn't know what she meant by "getting back home." It sounded like she hadn't been from Terra after all.

The stairs ended, and the elder motioned them into the room. It was dusty, and the roof was caved in near one corner. One of the walls was just gone, and they stuck to the intact side of the room to stay hidden.

"You are an angel," said the elder troll. "When you

185

can fly..." He pointed toward the broken wall. Carter carefully peeked around the corner and then sharply pulled back.

"The portal is down below," said Carter.

"Yes, I leave you here. We will distract them—you'll won't be able to miss it. Unrest is strong. The princess slaughtered a group of us this morning."

"Are you sure? This is a great sacrifice. I'm not sure we are worthy of it," replied Carter.

"We fight for our hearts and hope. You will give us more hope. Someday, we will get our home back. This," he motioned to himself and then at Carter, "is the beginning. Our legends say a Starwalker will save us."

"I can't make promises for her."

The elder just smiled and left through the dusty doorway. Carter leaned against the wall and let himself slide down. He looked up as Angie approached in wolf form.

"I'd lick you, but you look like shit. Are you really okay?" asked Angie.

Carter took a deep breath. "Yeah." He rubbed his shoulder, which kept taking the brunt of his battle damage. Even with magical healing, it might not heal all the way back to normal. He reached down to scratch the top of Angie's head just like Betha did. "Just how did we get into this mess?"

The wolf huffed. Inside his head, he heard her chuckle. *"We love Betha, who has a heart that is too big for all the worlds."*

Carter could feel his cheeks turn red, and he had no idea how to respond.

"Don't deny it. I see it even when you try to hide it."

He closed his eyes against the back wall, and an image of Betha came to mind—her sitting on one side of the campfire with a smile on her face. Yeah, he had feelings for her, but he wasn't sure what to do about it. He knew what he *wanted* to do, but just because he wanted to have a relationship with her didn't mean the timing was right.

The weight of the necklace brought his thoughts back to the here and now. Carter knew he shouldn't have accepted it, and he was going to be starting a new set of problems as soon as he handed it over. Yet, Betha would have done it. She would have taken the necklace even if the trolls hadn't offered to help. It was one of the things that drew him to her. She wanted to help everyone.

"Hopefully she's safe," muttered Carter.

"I pray to the fates that she is."

"Now, we wait." He glanced around the space. "You should see if there are some close shadows you can get us to."

The wolf padded toward the wall, looking for a way out of this mess.

ANGIE WISHED she knew how all of this was going to work out. Sending Betha away had definitely been the correct thing to do. While the group of them had put in a ton of training in the weeks after the funeral, it wasn't like the training that Carter and Angie had. Years trumped weeks of training, no matter how intense.

Still, Angie had to give Betha credit. She held up to the electric thing the princess had. Angie never would have said that Betha could hold up to torture. But she had until one of them had been threatened. This was something they would need to discuss once they got out of here.

She peeked around the stone wall. The portal was made out of flat red stones that were stacked on top of each other. Tall dead trees flanked it on either side. The sun wasn't high in the sky, but Angie didn't know how it would move. As she had learned on this trip, each freaking world was so different. You couldn't assume anything.

Already she was kicking herself for not taking any foreign languages. Everyone had always said she would regret not learning any, and here she was, wishing she had. One point to her parents and Grandpappy.

Then again, who thought they would be in the Fourth Circle of hell running from a crazy demon princess and the king of hell? You couldn't make this shit up.

She focused on the trunks of those trees. She could make it work. Right now, there was too much activity around the portal with demons coming and going. They would need the planned distraction from the trolls to make it through. Plus, once they were on the other side, she would need to quickly find a spot to take them away from the demon encampment. Based on intel from the gargoyles, each of the portals to hell had demonic camps right in front of them on Sky World.

"*The biggest battleground is on the other side, right?*" asked Angie.

"Yes, I think this is the one the angels are fighting at. The demons have built a pretty stable camp, complete with a wall."

"*So we will need to immediately flee.*" Angie padded away from the wall and sat down next to Carter. "*How was the shadow plane?*"

Carter shivered next to her. "Horrible. Darkness and existential dread. You feel nothing. All that you are is what is inside your head. If I ever piss you off, just kill me —don't leave me there."

His emotions came across the bond, and Angie didn't know how to respond. "*I'm sorry.*" She nudged him with her snout. His hand came up, and he patted her on the head.

Carter pulled his hand back. "Sorry, I didn't mean to keep petting you. And it's okay. It was the only way to get away. You did great thinking on your feet."

"*I don't mind. When is this distraction going to happen?*"

"In an hour or so, I'd guess. They need to spread the word. He said we wouldn't be able to miss it—I'd take a *cat* nap if I were you." Things were tough, and his joke wasn't very good, but he couldn't hide his slight grin. Maybe they'd survive after all.

THE PRINCESS TAPPED her foot impatiently. One of the hellhounds was sniffing around the prison cells. He kept leading them to a space in the center cell and then whining.

"We get it. What about anyone else?" asked Typhon. His voice was a deep growl as he pointed to the other cell. The hound moved to the rightmost cell and kept his nose to the ground. He traced a pattern on the floor and then took off racing down the hall.

Finally, they were getting somewhere.

Time was ticking, and she was doing all she could to remain calm. "I am going to greet the king. Report your findings."

The walk back up the stairs to ground level was the time she needed to wrap everything under her calm exterior. The order was accomplished. Typhon would find them, and this would all work out. She needed the king to go back to the other world as soon as possible if her plans were to work out.

She was the princess of hell. Nothing would stand in her way.

The dusty air greeted her as she reached the outside. The red stone and clay around this portal were frustrating. It created so much dust in the wind. The whole receiving area was compacted clay with broken buildings surrounding it. Most were used to temporarily hold soldiers before they were sent through. The slaves were kept in a few ramshackle buildings farther away.

Guards walked around the perimeter, but any slave that made a dash toward the portal was either shot with an arrow or taken down by hand. Dead trees flanked the doorway to the Seventh Circle. If this were her world, she would remove the deadwood.

The portal glowed, and two lieutenants walked through. Both had wings jutting from their shoulders and horns protruding from their foreheads. The twins reported directly to her father. They were two of the best warriors in their realm. They fought hard to move up the ranks together. The fact that they had gargoyle blood didn't slow them down. In fact, it had been a major advantage, they could pass as gargoyles from a large distance. The king wanted more demons who could fly as well as them, which was his loudest excuse for this invasion.

Anything to make the stand-still war with the angels go better. A different circle of hell had a portal directly to the angel world. They had been pushed out of that world, but her father didn't want to give up.

It was another one of those pipe dreams. The princess smiled at the twins, flashing her sharp teeth. They merely nodded at her since her ranking was only slightly higher than theirs. The crown on her head showed as much. Yet, she had taken over another land— her brother's. The increases in her power and influence were immense, and she wasn't sure how much higher she was above them now. Her speed and abilities on the battlefield had been on par with theirs. But she knew a secret about the twins. It was a dangerous secret, and one she guarded—if one was injured, the other was weakened. Hence the way they stuck together religiously.

"He is on his way, Princess," announced the right twin.

"Good, seeing the king is a welcome treat," she replied with as much sincerity as she could fake.

Both stared at her before turning back to the portal.

It would be great if Typhon showed up with good news right about now.

The portal sparked red and then the king walked through. The soldiers patrolling dropped to their knees immediately. Almost every demon in the area did as well. Immense power rolled across the air, and even Akeldama fought the urge to kneel.

Again, this pointless show of false respect was useless. All of the demons across this village were now on their knees. Completely useless, and a great opportunity for the insufferable slaves of this world to do something stupid and troublesome.

The princess noted that the twins had kept standing as well. That was new. All of the fighting must have increased their powers. That was dangerous.

The king stood just a few feet away from the portal, a deranged smile on his face. He only had six inches of height on her, but the exaggerated crown of spikes on his head gave him a few more. Short, dark red hair and glowing black eyes defined his features, while the pitch-black armor completed his royal fighter look. His skin was pale, and his fingers ended in blood-red claws.

The crown on his head grew out of his skull, showing all who laid eyes on him that here was the king of the demons. Eventually, it would fall off when an heir was considered worthy by the throne itself. The one on her head had been given to her months ago.

It was the first time he had called her daughter.

Every time they conquered a world, his power increased. The same happened to her when she had been given a second world to rule. Once she had taken over a third world, persuasion had become a power of hers. Each new world meant more power. The rush was addicting but she would resist.

"Daughter." The word rocked her, and she stepped forward, head held high.

"My king."

"Did you do as I say?"

"Yes, I caught the Traveler and brought her here." Movement caught her attention out of the corner of her eye. The guard from the prison kneeled on the packed clay, facing them. He bowed deeply to the pair of them and waited to rise. The king glanced at her.

"Report," commanded the princess.

"The Traveler has escaped, Princess," said the guard.

She knew instantly—Typhon had done this. He had given her a scapegoat.

Her expression froze over, as was expected. The guard remained in the bow. Her sword flashed before anyone could respond, and his head tumbled to the dust below.

"I abhor failure," she said. Inside, she was shaking. She prayed she was giving off cold vibes on the outside. Power built up around the king and she tightened down her emotions. She could taste his anger in the air, and could only hope her swift punishment of the scapegoat would temper his wrath.

Shouting and the sound of fighting caused her to turn and look away from her father. Typhon appeared by her side, and the twins took up positions next to the king.

"My King, my Princess," said Typhon through heaving breaths. "The slaves are revolting. Several soldiers are dead." He pulled his own weapon to protect his king.

EIGHTEEN

Carter watched the scene below carefully from behind the broken wall. Angie peered out from a broken window. It was a clearer look, and she could stay invisible in the shadows far better than Carter could.

"*Is that the King?*" asked Angie.

"He is wearing a crown," deadpanned Carter.

The figures below were having some sort of discussion when a demon approached. Then his head went flying.

Angie, still in wolf form, snorted. "*I think that was the guard that gave Andrea the keys.*"

Carter leaned back inside the room, wondering when the signal would happen.

"*Another demon appeared, and something is happening by the troll's house that we were in,*" Angie mentioned.

An explosion sounded from a nearby building, and Carter was glad for the stone wall surrounding them as it shook. "What was that?"

Angie didn't reply for a moment, then sent, "*I think*

that's our signal." She rushed over to his side. "*Are you ready to go to the shadows?*"

Before he could respond, Betha appeared in his head.

"*What the fuck?*" they both asked in pure astonishment.

BETHA FOCUSED on the portal that led to the world her Anchors were being kept on. She needed to rescue them, and so she would. Somehow, she was going to pull this off. She slipped into the in-between.

"I need to head back, I need to get my friends," she told the friendly presence in that space.

As soon as the words were out of her mouth, she was stepping into dust. Betha stared in shock. Smoke filled the air. No one was paying attention to the portal, but there was a group of demons with their backs to her. Light flicked from the heads of two of them, and Betha thought they might be crowns.

"*What the fuck?*" echoed in her head.

"*I'm saving you,*" answered Betha.

"*Hide behind that tree! Hurry!*" sent Angie.

Betha noticed the two dead trees next to the portal and hustled over. She wasn't as quiet as she would have liked. Before she could second-guess what was going on, Angie emerged from one of the tree's shadows, dragging someone. Carter quickly climbed to his feet and grabbed Betha's hand.

"*We need to get through the portal,*" he said.

Chanting echoed around the space, but it was too

quick for her to catch what was being said. Carter yanked her toward the portal, and as she glanced around the courtyard, her eyes locked with the princess'.

"The Traveler!" Her voice was louder than the chanting. "Get her!" She pointed directly at them, and Betha flinched. The demons near the portal dashed their way, but she was yanked backward through the simmering light. Betha landed on her rear, staring up at the portal that they had just come through.

"We need to move," whispered Carter.

Betha reached out and focused on closing the portal. As soon as her fingers touched it, it froze. The sparkles inside stopped moving. "I got this, guys."

"*That's not the problem,*" said Angie inside her head.

Betha glanced over her shoulder to see what was going on. Her eyes grew wide, and she almost let go of the portal. The skies were the bright blue of the gargoyle world, but tents surrounded the road leading from the portal. Campfires burned here and there. Not to mention all of the demons milling around. All staring at them.

"Well, fuck," said Betha.

A flash of bright white fire went up in the sky just passed a wall of broken rock surrounding the demon camp. Dark figures rose in unison in the air, heading right toward them. A loud horn sounded across the camp, and all of the demons turned toward the noise. Several took off toward the wall.

"*Those are gargoyles!*" exclaimed Angie.

"It must have been a signal!" answered Betha.

A group of demons launched arrows, but the gargoyles stayed too high. The wave of gargoyles kept coming, flying high above the battlefield in force. They rained arrows down on the demons.

Betha glanced around to find Angie, but she was gone. The marker in her head was jumping around from shadow to shadow. Carter was fighting hand-to-hand with a demon around ten feet in front of her. He disarmed the demon and took the sword for his own.

"Hold that portal," ordered Carter.

A gargoyle headed for her, surrounded by three others. His wings beat in the midday light. He didn't engage at all, only dodged the demons' arrows. Suddenly one of the gargoyles plummeted to the ground, taking an arrow meant for the central figure.

But the one in the lead kept going. Finally, he was close enough that Betha realized who he was—Derrik flew directly at her. Her fingers pressed harder into the air surrounding her hand and the portal. She must not let go.

"Betha! Hold it!" he shouted.

Finally, his wings stopped flapping, and he glided to his feet next to her. "It is time." He pulled a dagger from his belt and sliced it down his hand, then his arm. "It was an honor to meet you, Starwalker. I won't forget you. Or what you have done."

He thrust his arm into the frozen portal. "It's time to let go, Betha,"

"But...but...You're going to..."

"I am going to protect my people." Derrik said softly, almost reverently. He gave her a bright smile. "I am ready."

Betha released her grip. The portal flickered, but then

blue light spilled out from where Derrik was touching it. The bright blue light radiated from the portal, blinding her. The portal reached out to him and her. The image of the tattoo painted on his chest flashed inside her head.

"I give all that I am to protect this portal, this connection to the heart of hearts," said Derrik.

It was the same as when she had created the Anchor bonds. Bonding to the portals was like an anchor bond. Then the light vanished. Betha blinked several times to get her sight back. The portal glowed a light blue. Derrik was gone—nothing remained of him. Tears came to her eyes, and Betha didn't know what to do.

"Betha!" Carter grabbed her, pulling her away from the portal. He shoved her into a gargoyle's arms.

"I have you, Starwalker!" said a gruff voice. Rough hands pulled her close.

"Angie! Carter!" she screamed.

"Go! I'm coming!" answered Carter.

Betha could feel Angie already heading away from the portal. The gargoyle jumped up and took her to the air. Additional gargoyles surrounded them, and she saw white wings nearby. Carter flew near them.

Arrows whooshed into their ranks as they fled. A few hit gargoyles nearby, sending them falling from the sky. Down below, she could see the army that had waited for them. Inside her mind, she tracked Angie crossing a giant no-man's-land. All of the gargoyles were heading across open ground toward a different group of tents.

The gargoyle holding her flinched as something struck him—an arrow stuck out from the back of his leg. "I will get you there!" he said, determination fighting with pain in his voice. They flew lower and lower to the ground before they finally landed. The shaking gargoyle set Betha down before someone helped him limp away.

"Betha!" Carter pulled her into a hug. The spot in her mind that was Angie moved closer and closer. She was making larger jumps as she vanished and reappeared. "Why the hell did you come back for us? Don't ever do that again!" He pulled away and stared at her. "What were you thinking?"

The giant black wolf walked out of the shadows. She shifted from wolf to human and almost tackled Betha, who ignored the fact that Angie was completely naked. "Thank the fates! What Carter said."

"I thought you were still captured." Betha squeezed Angie in the hug before pulling away. "I came to rescue you."

"We were getting there. We had it," answered Angie.

"Well, how was I to know that?"

"Next time give us time to work," added Carter. He stood off to one side, shaking his head.

"How was I supposed to know what time it was?" asked Betha. Then she stared at Angie. "Did you take Carter through the shadow realm? How is that possible?"

"Necessity," said Angie

"Did it work, Starwalker?" asked a familiar voice.

Betha pulled out of Angie's hug. Her eyes landed on Sir Samson. He looked tired with his dark hair hanging limply.

"Do you mean Derrik?" asked Betha.

"Yes, did he bind to it?" The hopeful expression on the gargoyle's face almost broke her.

Betha nodded slowly. Her thoughts went back to that moment. She knew how to bind someone to the portals now. Derrik's sacrifice had shown her the way.

"Are you certain?" asked Gero. The elder joined Sir Samson.

"Yes, Derrik protects that portal. He is serving his people in the way he chose. Anyone who means your people harm will be stopped now," answered Betha with authority.

A cheer went up at her reply. Several people started talking about strategy, and Carter grabbed her hand again. "Let's find somewhere to clean up and get Angie clothes."

"It might be a little chilly right now," answered Angie. "Just a smidgen."

Carter talked to someone, and they pointed him toward a tent.

"We still have one more portal to go," whispered Betha. One last portal was bright red inside her head.

"That is a tomorrow problem. Hell, we literally just escaped hell. And closed a portal to hell. Like, we can take the rest of the day off once we get to the main camp," said her friend, shivering slightly.

Sounds of people celebrating flowed across the camp. "I guess you are right," Betha replied.

"Of course I am," answered Angie.

Fireflies drifted around Betha as she opened her eyes. Darkness and stars flickered overhead as she let herself completely relax. The tension in her shoulders melted away. She knew where she was. This was not a strange place any longer. Betha understood it was somehow connected to the in-between. The grass underneath her was cool, and she stared upward into the dark sky. Her thoughts kept circling.

Derrik was gone. And it stung.

She knew it had been coming, but it still shocked her. It had felt sudden. Add it to the events that had happened right before, and Betha did not know how to handle all of this. Betrayal, kidnapping, torture. How does one get over these types of experiences?

The fireflies above her grew brighter and some landed on her chest. It almost felt like when her mother would rub ointment on her when she was sick. Surprisingly, it helped. She let the tears trickle out. They weren't just for Derrik, who would never fly again. They were for her and Angie, Carter, and the gargoyle child that almost died. For Parian who lost a wing. All of the gargoyles who rose into the air to stop the portal from ever spilling demons again. Especially for the ones that fell from the sky, crashing below in the ultimate sacrifice.

All of this heartbreak, and for what? Because a king decided he should rule more than one world.

Light washed over her side, and Betha glanced down. The knife appeared in her hand, glowing just like the fireflies.

"I guess that's one thing we agree on, huh?" Now she was talking to a knife. Her mark glowed brighter in response. When it dimmed, Betha realized it was different. She sat up suddenly, and fireflies darted away at the movement.

It wasn't just the flickering light. The mark had changed—the compass rose had another behind it. It was faded but definitely there. The shadows from Angie and the wings from Eric and Carter were offset now. Layered behind the additional image.

Betha had anchored to the knife somehow. Genessa hadn't been telling a story. It was for real. That was another mystery she didn't know how to handle. Kyra's grandmother made her promise to come back and mentioned Kyra had made mistakes. And clearly, there was a lot Kyra hadn't told her. Soon, she thought, she'd have to fulfill that promise. After her friends were safe.

CHAPTER

NINETEEN

Betha snapped awake when she felt something touch her hand. Her fingers closed around it automatically, and the cool texture brought the knife to mind. Betha brought her hand up, and there it was—the knife that was supposed to be hidden inside her fancy boot. The boots were right next to the animal furs she was sleeping on.

The knife had moved itself.

"You okay?" asked a sleepy Angie. She was next to her on the furs, not fully awake.

"I'm good. Get some more sleep."

Her dark-haired friend rolled over and was out again. Sunlight was just starting to drift into their tent. Betha reached out mentally and found Carter outside, talking to someone. Then there was the knife. It was in her head *and* her hand.

"*You need to stay hidden,*" she pushed at it inside her head. "*If the demons got a hold of you, that would be bad.*"

The knife pulsed light, then it was gone.

"Oh shit." Betha frantically grabbed her boots, but it wasn't in the hidden space with the feather. "*Where did you go?*" she asked the feeling of the knife in her head.

The response was just a pulse of safety. The knife could respond and teleport. Whoa.

"Okay, that's good," she muttered to herself. Since she had her boots already, Betha started to get ready. She pulled on the body armor, which was becoming her second skin, followed by her boots. For a moment, the pretty dress she had worn to the nightclub before all of this had happened flashed in her mind. Before demons had invaded Terra. It felt like it was a lifetime ago.

When she opened the flap to the tent, sunlight was peeking over the horizon. Bright streaks of orange lit up the blue sky, and it brought a smile to her face. Despite the early hour, the camp was still going at full speed. It seemed there were even more gargoyles, and she spotted a troll. Once she spotted the first troll, she started seeing the rest of them. They were taller than the gargoyles, and while those with green skin stuck out, others had a blueish-gray tone similar to the gargoyles. Those trolls, at a quick glance, could pass for bigger, wingless gargoyles.

There were way more trolls than she thought were going to come. From the council meeting so long ago, it seemed only a few were going to come to guard her as she helped the gargoyles. Now, it looked like every troll on Terra had come to do their part. Or at least a good amount of them.

Carter gave her a wave, and Betha smiled. Next to him was a woman with bright white hair and golden armor. It took her a moment to place the armor, but she had to be an angel. The only one who'd had armor like that had been Parian. Betha hadn't seen a female angel before. Carter motioned Betha over, and she joined them. Given all of the trolls and gargoyles, she expected to see more angels, yet this was the first.

"Betha, this is Eden. She is a healer with the angelic host here."

"I am so excited to meet you!" said Eden. She offered Betha her hand. "I have heard so much about you. You used angel fire. That is kickass!"

Betha took her hand and was a bit taken aback by how casual Eden was being. She sounded like she was from Terra. The questions paused in her head when she caught sight of someone she knew.

"Parian!" She couldn't believe her eyes, but she knew it was him. It had to be. "Parian, wait!"

The familiar angel turned when she called his name the second time. He paused walking and let Betha catch up to him. The angel next to him looked rather confused when Betha almost tackled her friend with a hug.

The words spilled out of her frantically. "What are you doing here? I thought you would be going home to your family. I am so happy you made it." Betha squeezed him tight, then pulled back, looking him over.

A chuckle was his first reply but then he replied, "It is good to see you as well. When you vanished, I had faith that you would find your way back to us. Your Anchors as well."

The angel next to Parian said something softly before walking away. Betha turned a little red as she stepped back. Manhandling him hadn't been a good idea, plus she had barged into their conversation.

"I didn't mean to interrupt you, it's just...Good news is good news, right?"

"Seeing friendly faces in war is always good." He gave her a bright white smile. "I understand. Ah, good morning Carter, Eden." Parian bowed his head slightly to both.

Betha turned and noticed that they had followed her. Her cheeks heated up and she shrugged at Eden. "Sorry to ditch you guys, but I know Parian from the journey here. I didn't know what had happened to him."

"Parian was who I heard about you from," said Eden. "His family has been my host family in the heavens. The only reason I am here is that he argued my abilities would be helpful. I am required to stay away from battle, though."

Betha nodded like she understood, but instead, she had a ton more questions about Eden. The term "host family" made it sound like Eden was a foreign exchange student. Betha let that go, hoping to figure it all out eventually, and shifted her attention back to Parian. "What about your wing? Did it get healed?"

He shook his head. "It won't heal until I head home for a substantial time. Right now, I am needed here."

The angel that had been walking with Parian before came back, carrying a couple of swords. He held them out to Parian, who nodded with approval.

"This is Casial, my apprentice. Casial, this is Betha and Carter." Parian held out one of the swords to Carter. "I heard you lost your blade in the hell world, and given your help with my wing, I offer you this blade."

Carter took the sword carefully before pulling the blade out. Parian continued, "It is an angelic weapon blessed with the power of the heavens. I hope it serves you well in the battle ahead." Parian turned back to Betha and he held out a smaller sword. "I had to ask around to see if anyone had any blades in your size, but Casial found one."

The younger angel gave her a smile and a wink.

"This is a beauty," said Carter. "I thank you for this. I will use it well."

Betha took the sheath from Parian. "I hope to not have to use it, but thank you." The gift was thoughtful and useful, especially since they were in the middle of a war. Yet, the thought of having to fight still didn't sit well with her.

Eden's eyes bugged out. "You don't fight?"

"Only when necessary," said Betha. Her mind flashed to killing the prince. "I am a healer, not a fighter. I will fight only if I need to."

"Wait, you heal?"

Betha chuckled. Part of her wished she could heal people. "Not the same way you do. I heal the connections between the worlds."

That statement hung in the air for a moment.

"Betha, Carter, it was great to see you both again. I need to get back to work. So much to do before the first wave." Parian gave her a hug and then headed off with Casial. Betha had to revise her opinion that all angels were jerks. Maybe only the ones on Terra were jerks.

"He's famous, you know," whispered Eden. "He is the best teacher in the heavens. He used to lead a host but retired to teach instead. No one could figure out why he volunteered to come, but I think I get it now." Eden glanced between Carter and her.

"Carter, Betha," called out a voice.

Betha turned to see Sir Samson. He looked weary—dust and dirt lightly covered his legs, and his eyes weren't as bright as they had been on Terra. He seemed to have aged a few years, but she supposed war would do that.

"I better get back to the healing tents. May the fates watch over you," said Eden.

"May fireflies guide your path," answered Betha automatically. She paused, wondering where that had come from. It was not something she had ever said, or heard, before.

Eden gave her a strange look, then nodded before heading on her way.

"You doing okay?" asked Carter. "The last couple of days have been pretty intense." His blue eyes studied her.

"Yeah, so much is going on." Betha clutched the sword tighter in her hand as they headed toward Sir Samson. He motioned them over to a gathering of folks near one of the larger campfires. Betha struggled to get the belt of the scabbard around her waist as they walked. Carter took it from her and quickly clicked it into place. He was so close to her that she held her breath for a moment.

"Thanks," she said finally.

"Of course. Looks like Garruk is here." Carter took a step back.

He was right. Betha hadn't noticed the giant green troll until now. His horns were coated in bright blue paint. His dark hair was braided in between his horns. Thick leather armor covered his chest. Two other trolls flanked him, and both looked prepared for a fight with axes on their backs. An angel with bright white hair and skin that was literally glowing was next. Gero, one of the elder gargoyles, was nearby. They were thankfully talking among themselves and not staring at her. Betha noticed that Carter's hand went to the long necklace still around his neck.

Sir Samson spoke up and motioned to them both. The conversations stopped, and all eyes turned to Carter and Betha.

"This is Betha, the Starwalker, and Carter, one of her Anchors," proclaimed Sir Samson. "Betha, this is Garruk from the council, and Zebadiah, leader of the angelic host here on Sky World. We are discussing the plan to protect the last portal. The hope is that if we can get it guarded, we can then eliminate the rest of the demons that are stuck here over time."

"Do you have any other gargoyles willing to bond with the portal?" asked Betha.

"The last candidate did not make it through the trails. We have warriors ready to take the trials, but we don't have the time. It took Derrik two weeks to prepare."

Betha felt Angie move closer to the gathering. She reached out to her and Carter within the bond. "*I think I can anchor someone to a portal. It was just like anchoring each of you, but I am not sure."*

"Put it out in the open," replied Carter.

"I agree," added Angie.

The glowing angel was watching her intently.

"I think I can anchor someone to the portal even if they haven't passed the trials," said Betha.

Sir Samson took a step back, his eyes wide. "That's possible?"

"I think so. I was there when Derrik bonded with the portal." Betha closed her eyes, hearing his voice and remembering the connection forming between his soul and the portal. She could feel the light blue portal in her mind map. "I understand why you have trials—to make sure they are worthy. The same thing happens with Anchors. It needs to be with someone worthy."

"I volunteer," answered Gero. The ends of his wings were tattered and he moved slowly even while on the ground.

"You won't make it to the portal," replied the angel, cutting off Sir Samson before he could speak. "My friend, you are old and fly slow, and the battlefield is going to be rough. The demons will do anything to hold this spot. It is the last reliable pathway into this world. Up until now, the battle has been rough and spread out, but nothing like we have fought before on other worlds. It will be now that the demon king's multiple routes into this world are closed. He is going to be desperate. And do not forget you are one of the last elders. Your wisdom is needed here." His words were cold across the campfire. Even Garruk looked taken aback by his words.

"I am sorry Gero, but I agree," whispered Betha. "I will do my best to test some gargoyles. How much time do we have?"

The angel nodded to her, accepting her support. "Garruk is going to lead ground forces across the dead area. The angels and gargoyles will attack together in the sky. The goal will be to clear a space to get you through. But we must do it soon—our enemies are using that last portal to stage more forces every minute we delay."

"*Can you use the knife?*" asked Angie.

Betha hesitated. "*I promised not to.*"

"*To who?*" asked Carter immediately.

"*I'll tell you about it later. I don't think using it is a good idea.*"

"You can talk to them in your head," stated Zebadiah. Betha nodded in reply. "We can use that. Carter can join those in the sky and keep us updated. You have a wolf with you as well. We can cover both ground and sky. We can have a singer near Carter to keep us informed."

"A singer?" asked Carter.

"They relay messages."

"We will guard the Traveler," growled Garruk. "We have sworn to protect our little friend to our dying breaths. We have brought many who want the honor of fighting by your side and helping our sky cousins. We even have a decoy." Garruk motioned to someone Betha couldn't see, and an orc popped out from behind one of the taller trolls. They were short like her, in armor, their sex unclear. The orc pulled out a wig the same color as her hair.

Immediately, laughter bubbled up inside of Betha, and she forced herself not to show it. The poor orc with a wig on. Betha did not know how to respond—the orc looked so proud of themself.

"That's a good idea," said Carter, struggling to keep the grin off his own face. "We need to get masks for their face. No one will notice from a distance. Angie can move Betha through the shadows as she did me. We just need to create shadowy spaces, like in a chain."

The laughter died down inside Betha at Carter's serious tone. It was his "listen up" voice he used in training. It was also the voice that made her swoon. Betha gave him a smile in thanks. Laughing would not have been good. Still, she sent that image of the orc to Angie through the bond. Maybe her best friend would think it was as funny as she did.

"I am going to test some volunteers to see if I can feel anyone worthy," responded Betha. "They don't need to go through the trials, but if they aren't worthy, the bonding will fail and they will die, which we want to avoid." She gave a nod to Carter and the others at the campfire. Zebadiah's eyes tracked her as she moved, and it was unsettling.

"What is that necklace?" asked Garruk.

Betha stopped mid-step and turned. Carter reached out over his head and pulled it off. Garruk stepped forward, his eyes narrowed. "Where did you get an elder's necklace?"

"From Magnestrial."

All the trolls at the campfire glanced at each other in confusion.

"Magnestrial was destroyed. Lost to us," came Garruk's soft reply.

"Magnestrial is on the other side of that portal," said Carter, gesturing in the direction of the portal Derrik now guarded.

The sound that came out of Garruk rippled through the air. Every single troll nearby turned in their direction. In his cry was pain, amazement, and rage.

"An elder troll helped Angie and me escape when I was wounded by the demons. They led us to a healer and eventually to a safe spot to find a way free. They stood up to the king and caused a distraction to help us through the portal."

"There are trolls on the other side?" Garruk's nostrils flared, and his shoulders heaved.

Carter nodded. He hesitated before adding, "They are slaves."

Another scream bellowed out of the troll, and Betha felt a wave of power. His body shook, but the scream trailed off, and he regained control of himself.

"I promised I would bring this necklace to you, Garruk, the Axe that Cleaves in Two. And that they would not be forgotten. That the trolls who were free on other worlds would know that their brethren still breathe and fight. They believe that someday the majestic forests will grow back and the hunts on the plains will ride again."

Garruk kneeled down next to Carter and bowed his head. Carter stood up on his tippy toes and placed the necklace over Garruk's horns and neck before stepping back.

"I am Garruk, the Axe that Cleaves in Two, and I hear our people's hopes and dreams. We will create those hopes and dreams. We will bring them to be." He turned away from Carter and the campfire and strode off toward the crowd. Each troll followed him as he passed.

In her head, Betha heard Angie ask, *"Did they really say all of that to you?"*

"In their eyes, they did," answered Carter.

CHAPTER

TWENTY

Gargoyles lined up to be tested, but Betha had no idea what she was doing. It didn't help that inside her head she kept hearing the scream from Garruk. It was heart-wrenching, and it tore at her soul.

The background noise was pretty intense from the camp. The sounds of people talking, training, and sharpening weapons made it hard to focus. Loud clashes kept coming, and it was hard not to jump. Clouds hung in the sky, and she hoped they would not get rained on. It did fit her mood, almost perfectly, but rain wouldn't help any of their efforts.

The line of gargoyles had grown, and the pressure inside her to get this right grew with it. Betha kept a smile on, but her hands shook, and her hair kept falling in her eyes. Each time she motioned someone forward, she tried to reach out and see if she could get a feeling for if they were worthy. But she didn't know any of these people, and it felt like she couldn't connect with them.

After the first two gargoyles, Betha wanted to throw up her hands.

"*I thought I could figure this out,*" whispered Betha to her Anchors.

A chuckle came from Carter, and it caused her to relax. "*You can figure this out. What do you do when you are using your powers? That's what you did with us, isn't it?*"

Betha stared at the gargoyle in front of her, then she started to shift from side to side.

"Starwalker, are you okay?" the female gargoyle in front of her asked.

"Yeah. Take a deep breath, okay?" She reached out to the in-between to see if the presence there had any response. Light sparkled at her fingertips as she touched the gargoyle. She froze, but Betha ignored it. Feedback came across her magic, but it wasn't a clear answer. A humming sound echoed in her head from the spot she associated with the knife, but Betha didn't know how to understand what it meant.

"Am I worthy?" asked the gargoyle.

Betha let her frustration get the better of her and responded without thinking. "Do *you* think you are worthy?"

The knife stopped humming in her head, and Betha snapped to attention. It was a pause in all of the noise that was happening around her. Betha waited for the answer. The gargoyle woman had light gray, almost lilac skin. Her horns were small, and she had deep purple eyes.

"That is a good question, Starwalker." She looked like she was thinking. "I want to say that I am worthy. I have led a good life, but my people are dying. I would do anything to stop that, including losing the sky. I would give up my wings, my family, and ever seeing my loved ones again. The fact that my people would continue because of my sacrifice would be enough. But I don't know if that makes me worthy."

The knife started humming again, and she felt like fireflies were inside her stomach. "The love for your people and your willingness to sacrifice what you are makes you worthy. I see the truth in you and name you worthy." The words felt right as she spoke them, and Betha let her shoulders fall. Each time she took a breath, that tension dissipated further.

The gargoyle smiled. "I hope to see you on the battlefield then. Maybe we can stop all of this senseless dying."

"What is your name?" asked Betha.

"Rasika."

"Where is your home?"

Rasika shook her head. "They burned it to the ground —it is no more. Only a few escaped from my village. I only made it because I was away delivering some extra food to the battlefront."

Betha didn't know how to respond. While she had lost her mother, this was so much more devastating. All of the people she lived near gone. "Fate dealt you a hard hand, and I am sorry."

From there on, Betha asked each gargoyle if they thought they were worthy. Most had really good answers, but some didn't have conviction. Others were empty—their eyes seemed to have no spark, and when she touched them, it was just cold. All she could assume was that the fighting was too much and that their hope was gone. Instead of turning them away, she tried to bring that flame of hope back. Though she didn't know what good she did, if any, it seemed like the least she could do was try.

Angie found her a few hours later, after she had touched more gargoyles than she knew what to do with. Emotionally, she was worn out, and everything inside her wanted to go hide under a blanket. So many hopeless eyes.

"Hey, you need to eat," said Angie.

Betha wasn't sure how many more gargoyles were in line, but she waved goodbye to them. This was a good excuse, and she was going to take it with both hands. "Yeah, I can't do too much more of this. How are things going with you?" Betha asked, hoping for some good news.

Angie shrugged. "The angels have been doing short loops of angel fire to keep the demons contained. It's quiet at the demons' camp, which is worrying people. The first offensive is starting soon." Angie's lips tightened, then she continued, "Carter really stirred up the trolls."

Betha bet he had. "I mean, you suddenly find out that the home you lost is right behind a doorway and your people are slaves. That would piss off anyone. Or anyone with a heart."

"Well, the trolls have giant hearts then."

Angie led her through camp and around some tents. This section of tents was filled with trolls. A giant fire burned, and they were painting lines on their faces, chests, and horns. Garruk was leading a meditation group off to one side. Each of the trolls in that bunch had bright blue paint covering their horns.

Everywhere she looked, trolls were sharpening swords, strapping on armor, and preparing themselves for battle.

"Holy fates..." whispered Betha, her eyes wide as they traveled over the group.

"Yeah, I didn't think there were supposed to be this many. There are probably a hundred trolls who all showed up to protect you and the gargoyles."

Betha shook her head. "I don't need any more protectors—I have you guys." The hopeless look from the gargoyle earlier came to mind. "They should be able to help free this world for the gargoyles, though."

Angie elbowed her lightly in the side. "Don't sound so worried. We will get that portal shut down, and they can do the rest. We have done this before, and we can do it again."

Betha tried to let her worry slide free, but it stuck around. The pep talk didn't help as much as she wished. Images of the dead gargoyles from the village attack haunted her. Would that be the trolls' fate as well?

CARTER WATCHED the battlefield from one of the boulders they used for lookouts. The camp for the angels was at the top of a steep hill, rising above the plains that surrounded them. It gave them a height advantage, and, given how flat the rest of the area was, a good viewpoint.

He watched the angels do aerial rounds in no-man's-land with angel fire. One angel took out a bunch of smaller demons that had been creeping forward. They seemed to be the same type of demons that had attacked Terra. More creature-like than upright.

"You are bonded with the Traveler," stated Zebadiah.

Carter had been wondering when the angels were going to approach him. Well, when Zebadiah was going to come by. He had already run into a few different angels in the camp. All were approachable and seemed friendly. But Zebadiah had been paying too much attention to Betha and him at the meeting. Something was up with the leader of the angelic host. Carter turned to give him his full attention.

"Yet, you are Seth's son. I am surprised that you would bond with her. I know he had plans for his twins," added the angel.

Carter couldn't help but chuckle. "Fate laughs at others' plans." Him becoming an Anchor had not been on his to-do list. Eric's, sure, but not his. But here he was, and he was glad of it.

"My host is always looking for those worthy of the battlefield. I have heard of your battle prowess." Zebadiah walked around Carter, looking him up and down like goods for sale.

Carter shrugged. "I have always strived to be the best I can be."

Zebadiah continued like he hadn't heard him. "Even Parian came to see what you were capable of." This time, the older angel paused walking.

"Parian has been very helpful. Traveling and learning

from him is a gift I will treasure," Carter replied. The sword at his side felt good, and he was shocked the angel had given it to him. It was an amazing weapon, one that Carter would try not to lose.

Zebadiah stopped and studied him with his deep green eyes. "You know they are watching."

Carter's mind raced to figure out who he was talking about, but he didn't come up with anything. Finally, he needed to ask, "Who?"

"The archangels."

Everything inside his head froze, and he had no idea how to respond. Zebadiah gave him a nod and jumped into the air. His wings seemed almost golden in the sunlight that was peeking between the clouds. A shiver worked its way up his spine. The archangels were not to be messed with. When Eric and he were little, Kellion would whisper bedtime stories about them. They were both bogeymen and the ultimate heroes, depending on the situation.

When Betha had received the feather, he had been concerned, but not a single angel had asked about it. And now they were being watched by the archangels?

Carter shook his head. Right now, getting distracted with theories wouldn't be helpful. They were headed into battle, and that had to be his focus. Joy flickered through the bond, and it pushed the rest of the confusion away. Betha was the source, and he smiled. That was another distraction he didn't need, but part of him really wanted it. Maybe she had found the coffee he had traded the trolls for.

BETHA SQUEALED IN JOY. "Is that coffee?" She stole the thermos out of Angie's hands.

"Yeah, Carter somehow got it. No idea how, so ration that," directed Angie.

Betha took a sip of the warm beverage. It was a little dark and bitter, but oh so worth it. The caffeine was going to hit her like a rock. It had been too long. Hopefully, it would give her the strength for what was ahead, along with the drive to keep going.

"He is amazing," said Betha.

"I know that. You should tell him."

Betha rolled her eyes and wondered what he was doing. Based on the info from inside her head, she could tell he was near the edge of camp. Yet, she wasn't sure what exactly he was doing. While she could reach out, she didn't want to interrupt him either.

The camp surrounding her was busy with movement and noise. Gargoyles, trolls, and angels were getting ready to head into battle. Folks who wanted food were quickly eating. Others were tightening armor. Everyone was checking their weapons.

A group of confident trolls headed in their direction. A female warrior took point—she looked like a hero out of a bedtime story. Her horns were massive and painted a deep blue. She wore thick leather armor that covered her chest and a leather pleated skirt that reached her knees. Two large swords were at her side, and the blue paint continued down her face and across her eyes.

"Traveler! I am Nesse, and we will be your first

guard." Nesse stepped to the side. Each troll behind Nesse had a shield. "Groups of us will create the dark spaces needed to move you quickly ahead. Each of us has the blue horns."

"That's smart," remarked Angie. Betha had to agree.

"Wolf!" Nesse called out, and Angie stood up.

"It's Angie."

"Wolf—uh, Angie—you saw our people, an elder?" asked Nesse.

She nodded. "He led us to safety. I didn't understand a single word he spoke."

"But you saw him, for real?"

"I did."

Nesse clapped Angie hard on the shoulder, who wavered under the pressure. "You are wolf-friend." All of the trolls hammered at once on their shields. "All of us mountain trolls will know your name. You honor us deeply by bringing news of our lost kin."

Betha's eyes grew wide. You couldn't make this stuff up. Who knew that trolls loved making dramatic statements so much? Too bad she didn't have any paper, and Angie had stashed her sketchbook somewhere. Betha wished she could write this down to remember it exactly later. Grandpappy would love hearing about this. Angie glared at her like she knew what she was thinking.

"We will get you and the Traveler to that gate," said Nesse. "The time is upon us."

"Good," said Betha. She nudged Angie. "The coffee is gone."

"You drank it all?" Angie turned toward her. "I told you to ration it!"

"Wolf-friend Angie, you like coffee?" interrupted Nessa. She thrust a canteen into Angie's face. "We drink it before battle! It helps make us strong!"

Angie accepted the canteen and took a swig. "*Oh goddess, it is so bitter,*" said Angie.

"*Now we know where Carter got it from,*" answered Betha.

"It's good, thank you," said Angie, handing it back to Nesse.

"Good! Time to move! We will hammer when it is time for you to shadow."

The trolls surrounded them, and Betha sent up a quick prayer to the fates. May we make it through this. May Sky World stay free. Watching the trolls surround them, she added one more prayer—may the troll world someday be free. The weight of everything came crashing down on her, and her resolve grew.

"*Carter?*" Betha hesitated, then continued, "*Good luck in the skies today.*"

"*I am headed your way, give me...*" The dot in her mind moved closer to her at a fast pace.

"Two seconds," he finished as he landed gracefully nearby. The sunlight caught his wings, and it took her breath away. He nodded at the group of trolls. Carter then wrapped her in a tight hug, and she breathed in the scent of pine. "You got this. A quick jaunt across the battlefield and closing the portal, then you need to get out of there." His arms tightened again, squeezing her hard against his chest, and she swore she felt him press a kiss to her hair before he pulled back. "I'll be flying, hopefully nearby."

"We will be fine." Betha tried to smile, but her thoughts kept repeating how close he was and that she should just kiss him. A horn sounded, and he stepped back. "You got this!" she said instead. Mentally, she kicked herself.

Carter gave her a nod and jumped back into the air.

"Smooth, Betha." Angie gave her one last smile, then tore off the shift she was wearing. A giant wolf took her place.

Now was the time.

TWENTY-ONE

Screams and sounds of fighting came from up ahead. Betha tried to block them out. The trolls created a tight circle around the two of them. They moved quickly, and Betha was thankful for her extra speed. If she didn't have it, she wouldn't be able to keep up. They blocked most of her field of vision, leaving her to look at lots of armor and green skin.

What she couldn't see, however, she could still hear. The screams and snarls of combat, the injured and dying. She could hear grunts of effort and the ring of steel on steel. The gargoyles and angels fought the demon horde, making way for the small troop. And, to her horror, something she hadn't noticed before—the smell of battle. The sharp iron stink of fresh blood, but also the brimstone and sulfur smell of the dying demons. Under it all, the wet, living smell of the mud, grass, and plants being trampled on this field of combat.

"Incoming!" called out Nesse.

The trolls surrounding them shifted. Nesse broke

forward, and Betha caught glimpses of the battlefield—a troll fought a demonic soldier with a spiked tail, a giant ball of white flames hit the ground near a group of demons, turning them to ash. Betha blinked at the bright light, and her fingers tightened on Angie's fur. All that mattered was getting to that portal, but Betha had no idea how much ground they had crossed so far, or how much farther they had to go. Angie padded beside her, staying within the circle of trolls. The group of them caught up with Nesse, and they spread back out.

"Wolf, you have two minutes!" said Nesse.

The trolls all around them twisted in one coordinated movement. A troll raised a shield overhead, creating shadows surrounding them. Angie poked her head out, looking across the field. Betha stayed put. She didn't want to see anymore. She knew she had to do this. She *could* do this for her friends, but it was like a tour through a nightmare.

"Hold your breath on three! One, two, three!" Angie clamped down onto her upper arm and yanked backward.

Darkness washed over her.

THE PLAN WAS brilliant since the demons had started aggressively attacking flyers across the battlefield. It seemed the demons had learned a lesson from the gargoyles getting Betha off the last battlefield. Angie would stay in wolf form, and they would hopscotch across the battlefield. Teams of seven trolls each had shields, and when they heard the hammer, they would create a space. No one knew if they would appear there, but the shadows would be there for two minutes. Angie's goal was to get Betha to that portal as soon as possible. It should have worked.

The fates laugh at well-laid plans.

Bright fucking burning light. In the one place there was always darkness, where light had not touched in memory, where Angie had never seen so much as a candle—Betha brought light. And it fucking hurt. Angie had to let go immediately as sizzling came from where she was touching Betha. Her mouth felt like it was on fire. A howl escaped automatically, rolling across the empty space.

To her shock, someone answered it. A howl rose up far away in the distance—a call to her pain. It was a call to come home. Her wolf knew what it meant, and every-thing in her wanted to respond. Angie froze. This was impossible. This whole thing was impossible.

Her focus was brought back to her task as the bright light next to her called out. "Angie! Are you okay? Angie!"

The sound carried across the darkness. Betha shouldn't be able to speak here. No one could speak here. Angie didn't know what was going on. They had to stick to the plan. They couldn't stay here. Instead, she braced herself and touched Betha, yanking her back out again.

The trolls surrounding them were different, and her mouth was freaking bleeding. The taste of blood rolled over her tongue, which felt burnt and blistered. Pain washed over her face, but she resisted shifting. Her healing would catch up. It had to.

"Angie, what was that?" asked Betha.

Angie didn't think she could do as many jumps as they were hoping. The trolls pulled in tighter around them. She could hear the fighting. A troll peeled off, and the space got small. Things must not be going well.

"Wolf, you need to go! We can't hold here," growled a male voice. "The decoy is dead!"

The thumping on the shields came again, very loud in her ears this time. Angie peeked out for any darkness across the distance. The smell of blood and pain was everywhere. She needed to get them closer. This was too far. Betha wouldn't make it.

Across the battlefield, she ignored the dead and realized just how many demons were on the field. A dark spot under billowing fabric caught her eye. It was far, but probably doable. It had to be. Gritting her teeth against the pain, not knowing what to expect, she prepared herself.

"*Deep breath!*"

"Angie, wait!"

Angie didn't pause. She yanked Betha back into the darkness. When the burning came, she didn't let go. Instead, she pulled Betha back to Sky World. This time, trolls did not surround them. Tent fabric was over their heads. A wooden staff held the tent open, but the back wall lay flat on the ground. It had been enough. Angie crashed to the floor. Her mouth was on fire, and the pain was more than she could stand. Her consciousness flickered.

∾

BETHA WAS YANKED out of the darkness again. This time there wasn't room to move, and she was on the ground. Cloth hung above them in a makeshift tent, and Angie whimpered beside her. Betha tracked the sound, and her stomach roiled—blood covered Angie's mouth. It looked like someone had held her friend's open mouth over a hot flame. Her wolf tongue was blackened and oozing a clear liquid, and the rest looked like charred meat.

"Shift Angie. Just do it," Betha said to her chosen sister.

The wolf shook, and the sound of bones crunching was loud. Betha stared into Angie's eyes as she changed. It took everything not to scream. Bones reshaped themselves under her skin, and the fur retreated, leaving pale skin behind. Angie panted, still shaking on the ground. Her golden eyes were full of tears, and Betha didn't know what to do.

Angie was never injured, not like this. Black marks still surrounded her lips, but it was no longer oozing. Her face looked okay if you ignored the blood.

But something definitely felt wrong. The hair was raised on her neck.

"What happened?" whispered Betha.

"You burned me in the darkness," Angie's words barely came out. "I don't think I can move."

Betha peeked out the opening of the tent. They were much farther back in the camp surrounding the portal— she could feel it behind them. Betha reached out, connecting with the portal. It was much closer than before. Demons were using it, but not many. It gave her hope that they could still do this.

"Can you stay here?" Betha asked.

"*Yes,*" Angie responded. "*I don't think any demons are nearby, but it's hard to smell anything right now. You need to keep moving.*"

Betha didn't want to leave Angie there by herself. It felt wrong. Everything inside her wanted to curl up next to her best friend and wait this out. The knife hummed in the back of her mind, reminding her of her duty. People were dying out there to get her closer to the portal. Derrik had given up everything to guard the last portal, and other gargoyles were flying about waiting to do the same.

She couldn't stay here. Betha was a Traveler, and she had a job to do.

"*Betha, it's okay. I will be fine,*" said Angie.

"Okay. I will be right back as soon as the portal is protected. Don't go anywhere."

Everything suddenly shattered inside her head. Pain rippled across the connection she had with the portal, then down the bond. Angie snapped a hand over Betha's mouth as her body shuddered. Her timing was perfect, and Betha screamed inside their heads instead of out loud. Screamed like she hadn't imagined anyone could scream.

TWENTY-TWO

Carter almost dropped from the sky. Pain rippled out from Betha. The first round had been from Angie, but he could deal with that. This was much, much worse.

"*The portal!*" cried Betha.

"What's happening?" asked Carter, both out loud and in his head.

"*Something is coming through. It's giant. Oh, fates!*" sent Betha.

"Carter, what's happening?" asked the angel beside him.

He had been assigned a singer to relay orders during battle. They could sing across large distances, letting angels even far away hear messages clearly, giving instructions in code that only other singers knew. It made sense, even though he did not understand the songs themselves.

"Something big is coming through the portal. Bigger than the portal."

The angelic singer opened his mouth, and music poured out. The angels at the front of the battlefield turned in midair as a unit. They headed directly toward the portal and poured angel fire at the opening in waves instead of spheres. Such action took a lot out of them and opened them to a flanking attack, but it was clear this was important.

It took everything for Carter to remain in the air. They were in the second wave that would be heading toward the battle. Half of the host was already doing passes of angel fire or fighting against flying demons. The air was filled with more flying creatures than he had ever seen. There were angels, gargoyles, and demons.

Betha and Angie were close to the portal. Closer than they were supposed to be already. They were behind the enemy's line.

Even from this distance, he could see something poking through the center of the portal. Giant claws, each the size of a person, pushed through, yanking at one of the sides. Something started squeezing through, impossibly large. Light reflected off of the black scales of the creature. Then claws were followed by a leg, a shoulder, then a head.

"What the fuck is that?" asked Carter.

The signer changed the song before cutting off. "That's a dragnus. Giant creature, breathes fire. It might be able to fly. I haven't seen one in person, though the ancient stories mention them. The king must be desperate. Tradition holds they are very hard to control, and it's as likely to turn on the demons as not when it's done with us."

"Shit, Betha and Angie are over there!" Carter pointed to the area to the right of the portal. There was plenty of space and not a lot of fighting going on nearby, but they were still way too close to that thing. Various tents were strung about in no particular order, and Carter could tell they were in one of them.

"I'll send a distraction," said the singer.

The head of the dragnus pushed out of the portal like a cat trying to wiggle its way through a space that was too small. The singer sang a very different song, with chirps and pops. Several gargoyles dashed to the ground near the various groups of trolls, then rose back in the air.

The whole battlefield shifted. The trolls on the ground all pushed forward to break the line of demons fighting. The head of the dragnus suddenly pulled back, and two quick demons flew out of the portal into the air. Once they were airborne, the portal glowed again, and the head was back. The dragnus tried to shove its shoulders through the too-small space. With each shove, Carter could feel something from Betha. It was barely there. She had to be blocking it from the bond, but it must be causing her immense pain, if the earlier scream had been any indication.

"Gargoyles are heading to the portal, along with trolls. They will watch for the Traveler. We need to close the portal before that thing makes it through," said the singer.

The two flying demons went right for the gargoyles in the air, pushing back against the advance. A gargoyle dropped from the sky.

"Shit, it's the twins," whispered the singer. Then he was sending another song into the chaotic battle.

"*Help is on the way,*" sent Carter to his family. He flew toward the tents.

~

PAIN WASHED OVER BETHA, and she barely remained upright. Whatever was trying to come through the portal was tearing it. She hadn't known that was possible, but here she was, learning again. This was a lesson she could have done without. Then suddenly, the pain vanished. At least she could now breathe.

"I think we need to move," said Angie. Her voice was soft but encouraging.

"To where?"

"The goal is the portal. I can get up."

"*Help is on the way,*" sent Carter.

"Can you shift back?" asked Betha. Her eyes roamed the inside of the tent, but there wasn't anything Angie could wear. It was a dirt floor with just the opening held up by three wooden sticks.

"I can try." Angie's face was still stark white, and dark circles were under her eyes. The fact she had moved as quickly as she had to stop Betha from screaming was a feat.

Betha kept her eyes on her best friend as she shook. The shift back into her giant wolf form took much longer than the shift to human. As Angie grew bigger, she hit the one stick holding the tent up. Betha rolled out of the way and saw the sky above her. She jumped to her feet and pulled out her sword.

Angie stayed under the tent, her form shaking. Pain and worry crossed the bond.

Betha nudged her with her foot. "Angie, are you okay?"

The shape shuddered again and grew smaller.

"I can't do it," cried Angie. The tent stopped moving. A few tents were still up around them, and Betha moved behind one of them. This looked to be a resting area, but the sounds of fighting were close. Betha didn't know what to do. How could Angie not be able to shift?

"Just rest, I will be right back," whispered Betha. She didn't want to leave Angie behind, but she could feel time was running short. Uneasiness settled into her gut. Betha peeked out from behind the tent toward where the portal was located. They were still a good distance from it, but much closer than they had planned to be so soon. Her eyes landed on it, and she quickly yanked herself back. Her heart pounded hard in her chest.

"*Oh my goddess. It's a freaking dragon,*" she pushed down the bond to Angie.

A gargoyle crashed into the tent beside her, wings and limbs going every which way. Betha glanced up in panic. She had forgotten the battle going on way above her head. High above her, she could see two demons flying about with swords, taking out gargoyles left and right. A group of angels was headed in that direction. Half split off toward the portal.

"*I'm coming!*" Carter's voice echoed through her head. His presence was coming closer. That wasn't the plan. Betha didn't want to draw the attention of the flying demons. The angels dove toward the demons, and they took off away from the gargoyles as angel fire flashed.

"Angie, we need to move," whispered Betha.

Angie slowly crawled out from under the tent. "That sucked."

"Let's suck somewhere else." Betha's put her arm around Angie. The sound of Angie's harsh breathing against her side grounded her. Bright white fire crashed into the tents that they had been hiding in, turning them to soot. The portal was close, but getting there was going to be tricky. It was located on a rock outcropping in the middle of the plains. Her eyes caught sight of the dragon, which had one shoulder, an arm with claws, and its head pushed through.

Betha kept her arm around Angie and led to near a rock that kept them both out of view. Angie slumped down next to her. A flash of purple landed next to them, and Betha stabbed. Rasika parried the blow.

"Careful, Starwalker."

"Rasika, sorry!"

She chuckled and moved closer to Betha. "What is that creature?"

"No idea, but it needs to move out of the portal."

A roar came from the dragon as it shoved forward. Pain rippled over Betha. She could feel it pressing against the portal. Her fingers tightened around the pommel of her sword. "Don't tear," she whispered. "You can hold."

Betha reached out to the portal and wished she hadn't. More pain rolled through her body, making everything shake. The portal was stretching. Slowly, but it was giving way. This must be one of the ways some of those smaller tears she had found were all stretched out. "You can hold." Betha pushed all of her hope toward the portal. Two others joined her mentally. One she recognized instantly as Derrik. The other had to be Magson. The three of them focused on holding back the dragon.

The ground shuddered as the dragon creature roared. That roar of anger was answered by another—a shout of many voices coming from the front line. The sound of a large group of people charging worried her. Betha struggled to look the other way from the portal, forcing her gaze back to the battle.

The connection with the portal almost broke, but it held as she took in the scene. Garruk was leading a band of trolls at full speed toward the dragon. Trolls had broken through the mass of demons. Feet pounding, they sped over the ground. The dragon pulled back and aimed. It opened its mouth and fire rolled out.

"Oh no!" she gasped. The brave trolls were going to burn.

Betha flinched, waiting for the flame to engulf the trolls. Somehow, bright white light came from a group of angels swooping down from the air in front of them. The angel fire hit the red hot flames of the dragon, and the flames shifted.

Garruk didn't even slow.

The fire flickered out, and the dragon pushed even harder against the portal. Betha, Derrik, and Magson pushed back. This would end here.

Garruk bellowed again and raised his great two-handed axe. Bright green light flickered from his eyes, and he grew bigger. The troll gained a foot of height, then two, and he sped up even more. One moment, he was still ten feet away, then he was suddenly in range.

He swung his axe down, and the dragon screamed. Blood spewed everywhere. The pressure on the portal was suddenly gone.

Betha tugged on Rasika's arm. "We need to move, now!" she said.

The portal flickered again, but Garruk kept swinging. His nine-foot form stood guard right in front of it, but he did not pass through. Any time something tried to pass, he would swing at it. True to his name, more often than not, that thing would be cleaved cleanly in two.

A group of demons came out of nowhere from the opposite side as Betha and Rasika charged the portal. Betha stumbled but kept running as she kept her eyes focused on her destination. If she could hold the portal, Garruk could focus on the demons. They just needed to be faster. More trolls poured forward and cut the demons off. Betha held her sword in one hand, reaching for the portal with the other. Finally, her fingers touched the swirling golden light. Everything within the outcropping stopped.

Garruk's wide eyes met hers. "Traveler! You have come!"

Angie had no idea what was wrong with her. Whatever Betha had done in the shadow plane had fucked her up.

It was the first time she had ever tried to shift and failed. Her wolf had refused. Flat out refused. It was still in pain, whatever had happened, and she was healing much slower than normal.

And now she was naked on a battlefield, huddled against a rock while her best friend tried to close the portal on an evil dragon of doom.

A horned green figure headed her way, and her shoulders relaxed a smidgen. The ground was rough underneath her rear, and everything hurt. She had no idea why her healing factor wasn't doing anything.

"You don't look so good, wolf-friend," said Nesse.

"I don't feel so good," answered Angie. It took everything she had to keep her head upright. A battle was happening in the sky, and it was one the trolls weren't part of. Nesse had both swords out, staring at the moving figures above. Two flying demons were more than holding their own, taking out as many gargoyles as they could. They had to keep dodging the groups of angels pursuing them, but clearly, they were talented and used to working as a team.

Angie kept her eyes on them but froze as they suddenly headed toward the portal.

"Betha, flying demons incoming!"

Gargoyles blocked the demons midair to keep them contained above the battlefield, and Angie relaxed a little. At least they had help. That help was costing them dearly, though, as she saw another gargoyle cut down by the fiendishly effective pair of demons.

"You need to close that portal!" she sent her friend.

The feeling of being lightheaded increased, and

keeping her eyes open was getting difficult. She focused, trying hard. If she couldn't fight, at least she could spot. She could help. She only had to stay conscious.

"It is time. Rasika, are you ready?" asked Betha. She didn't know what else to do. On the other side of the portal, she could feel creatures pushing on it. They were trying to come through, and Betha knew that she, Derrik, and Magson couldn't keep them back much longer.

Rasika's eyes darkened, then she nodded. "Let's do this. What do I do?"

Garruk stared at the two of them intently, and Betha ordered, "Keep the demons back, Garruk!"

"I am sorry, this is going to hurt," Betha said. It had to be just like Derrik. Betha slashed Rasika's arm with her sword. The cut was deep, and blood poured out of the wound. Betha's heart pounded in her chest, and she ignored the slight panic she felt. This would work. She knew how this worked. "Repeat after me: I give all that I am to protect this portal, this connection to the heart of hearts."

Rasika thrust her arm toward the portal, and Betha let the portal flicker open. Rasika's bloody arm passed through, and the portal froze again. "I give all that I am to protect this portal, this connection to the heart of hearts."

Blue light spread from the connection, and Betha could feel Derrik and Magson there. The knife hummed in the back of her head, and this time, she could tell it was with approval. They were on the right track. This would work. It had to. Betha nudged the energy from the portal toward Rasika.

"Mom?" asked Derrik softly. The words vibrated inside her head. Betha's eyes grew wide as she turned toward Rasika.

"I am here, my son," whispered the lilac gargoyle. Rasika winked at her, then vanished. Her body dissolved into white light. Betha stumbled backward as the connection from the portal was cut off. A giant green hand caught her before she hit the ground—Garruk kept her upright.

That had been Derrik's mom, the whole reason he had decided to become a Guardian. He had thought she died in the village. Now she was a Guardian too, and they were together again.

Garruk gave her a nod, but she noticed he was crying. Tears rolled down his face, and Betha didn't know what to say. His other hand touched the portal but didn't go through. Once she was stable, Garruk let her go. He turned toward the fighting that was still going on. Then the giant troll took off, axe raised high.

Betha made her way back to the rock where she had left Angie. Everything seemed to be moving in slow motion, and she had no idea why. Her friend was still there, and Nesse stood guard.

"You look worse," Betha said to her dearest friend in all the worlds. Angie looked even paler than before.

"I don't feel so good," responded Angie.

"I think we need to get some food in you as soon as

possible," Betha said, looking up. She didn't know what else to offer.

The battle was still going on. Despite getting the last portal protected, leaving the remaining demons cut off, there was still a small army of the fiends between them and the safety of the camp. Betha had no idea how they would get back safely, especially since it was clear Angie couldn't move quickly. Everyone was focused on their orders. Thankfully, Nessa was there. Betha wasn't sure if she could swing her own sword—binding Rasika to the portal had taken a lot out of her, and everything felt like jelly.

A big part of her wanted to cry. Angie was hurt, Derrik was gone, and Rasika had joined him. The trolls were this close to their home world but couldn't cross. Not yet. And the battle was still going on. People were dying, and for what? Greed? Power?

And she knew that, tired though she was, her day was not yet done.

TWENTY-THREE

Carter had been studying the twin demons flying in the air, each armored and with swords. A group of angels had gotten them with angel fire, but their armor had reflected it. Angel fire burned through everything, he'd thought. Today he'd learned differently.

The twins slowly started making their way back toward the portal, which meant back toward where Betha and Angie were hiding. There was something about how they moved. The singer beside him changed the song again before pausing.

"I am going to help fight the twins," stated Carter. His eyes narrowed as he kept his gaze on the two in the air.

"Are you sure?" the singer asked.

"They move like me and my brother. We need to separate them." An idea popped into his head. "Angel fire. Use angel fire to create a wall." Carter took off flying across the sky.

The singer changed his tune as he followed, and Zebadiah joined them.

"What do you see?" asked the head of the host.

"They are moving like they share senses. My brother and I can sometimes slip into that." He didn't add that it was especially true since they had bonded with Betha. "We need to separate them or darken their senses."

The angel didn't reply for a moment but then nodded. "I know what to do. We need some time." He called across the battlefield, and the singer's song cut off. His face went white.

"Are you sure, sir?" asked the singer.

"Yes, we will clear the area. Carter, get your people away from there."

Carter took off. He had no idea what the host was going to do, but if Zebadiah wanted Betha and Angie out of there, Carter would get them out of there.

"Betha, Angie, retreat!"

He flew toward the twins, trying to keep track of where Betha and Angie were on the ground. The twins were getting too close to them. His sword was out and in one hand. He would have to get closer to them to be any sort of threat, though. His attention was split, keeping an eye on Betha and Angie, and it didn't take long for him to reach the group of gargoyles that was trying to contain the twins in one space. Unfortunately, as brave as they were, gargoyles were hunters, not warriors for the most part, and the coordination of the twins had them outmatched. Only their numbers had kept the twins contained so far, and they had paid a terrible cost.

Carter got there just in time to block a blow that

would have split the head of a gargoyle. His sword held firm and sparked with angel fire. The demon barred sharp teeth at him.

"Let's dance, bird boy!" said the demon.

Carter's eyes grew wide as the demon spoke his language. "You're on!" he growled back.

He tried to keep an eye on the other twin as well. He kept thinking about what he and Eric would do. If he could predict their movements, he could hold them. His free hand glowed with fire, and he tossed it at the one in front of him. It gave him a moment to block the other twin who was trying to stab at his back. The gargoyles tried to dart in with their spears as a distraction. He just needed to buy the angels some time to do whatever they were doing. At the very least, the twins weren't retreating anymore. He was holding them, and they weren't slaughtering gargoyles.

Then he had two swords coming at him again. They had to be talking to one another. Carter blocked one and summoned more angel fire. It created a wall on one side of his body. The heat caused sweat to break out on his forehead. Lightening flickered against his wall, but it didn't make it through the angel fire. He kicked at the one he was blocking, pushing the demon back several feet. Then he stabbed out through the angel fire at the other twin.

The blow was sudden and as fast as he could make it. His blade bit deep—clearly the demon hadn't expected the strike. The angelic sword drove into the demon's ribs. The one he had knocked back screamed in unison with the one who had been stabbed. Carter moved to attack but noticed the angels flying toward them and the gargoyles fleeing. He had bought enough time—now he had to save his family. He spun and dove in Betha's direction.

CARTER'S SHOUT moved Betha into action. Time seemed to switch back to normal speed. She jumped up and put her arm under Angie's shoulder. "We need to retreat, Nesse. And I get the sense that it should be as fast as possible."

The troll glanced down at the two of them and slid her swords into their sheaths. "I'll take wolf-Friend." Before Angie could reply, Nesse slung the naked girl over her giant shoulder. Betha didn't know what to say as Angie's bare ass pointed sky-high, draped like a sack of grain over the troll's back. Given that Angie didn't say anything, she knew things were very wrong with her friend.

Betha yanked her own sword out and took the lead. To her surprise, Garruk joined them, calling to others. They were not the only ones fleeing the area. All of the trolls and gargoyles were leaving as quickly as possible. Betha didn't understand. The portal was guarded now, but there were still plenty of demons on this side of it. Though maybe they were hoping the demons would flee while they had the chance?

Even in the sky, movement was everywhere. The two flying demons were taking out as many gargoyles and angels as possible. For every one that dropped, though, it seemed two took their place. It was like a group of ants swarming. It didn't make sense.

Then Carter flew forward, moving faster than she had ever seen, distracting and holding the twin demons at bay. Her heart was in her throat, and she tried to keep moving. Fear for Carter ate at her.

Two angels, in silver armor instead of gold, flew forward. The twin demons didn't notice as a group of gargoyles kept them occupied. A bright light seemed to gather around the angels. It grew more intense, then they screamed. It was a sound of pure horror. The bright light streamed outward, and Betha couldn't move. Even as far away as they were, she couldn't move. Something inside of her screamed danger, that they needed to flee, but her feet were rooted to the ground. The gargoyles tried to scramble away, but many fell.

Betha couldn't look away. The light engulfed anyone still in range. Gargoyle, demon, angel, it didn't matter. Not everyone had moved out of the area in time. All in the blast radius clutched at their ears. Yet the sound did not stop. Their wings did, however. The entire group tumbled down, falling through the air.

Everyone surrounding her stared in shock at the angels above. All of a sudden, it was as if a switch had been flipped. The demons that were left pivoted toward the portal as quickly as possible. The portal flickered as they passed back to the Fourth Circle of hell. The voice inside of her screaming to run softened, then vanished.

The group of gargoyles who had been fleeing reversed course and headed after their falling allies. They flew frantically, recklessly, diving to catch friends who fell from the sky, while dodging those demons that were hitting the ground solidly.

Carter landed near Betha and blocked her vision of the sky. "Are you okay?" he asked. His words were rushed, and he seemed shaken as his eyes traveled over her, searching to make sure that she was all right. He was okay, and she could breathe again, but she wasn't sure if the demons had gotten a hit in. She didn't see anything, but he was good at hiding things like that.

Her focus was on him and not what he was saying. She nodded absentmindedly. "I think so—"

Her sentence was cut short as he grabbed her around the waist and pulled her close. His lips met hers. She was utterly surprised, and for a moment, she was too stunned to kiss him back. But it was only a moment, then her lips softened, and she gave it all she had. She'd wanted this for months, and now she knew he had too. Fireworks went off in her brain, her belly, and her heart. Time froze for the second time.

Betha slowly pulled away after what seemed like hours, remembering they were in the middle of a battle, but he only tightened his arms around her.

"I was so worried about you," he muttered into her hair.

"That was something," whispered Betha. It had happened. They had kissed. It was for real.

"Something good, hopefully."

"Yeah, uh, that was good." The glowing spark that was Angie flickered in her mind, breaking the moment. "Uh, not that this isn't important—it is important—but Angie is broken."

"Wait, what?" Carter turned around, but Betha realized that Nesse must have kept going.

"Something happened in the shadow plane. I don't know what, but she's not doing well."

~

AKELDAMA WANTED TO SCREAM. Instead, she stood at attention watching her father scream. In her childhood, she had perfected the art of keeping a bored expression on her face. She made her body relax as she waited for the king to calm down. Typhon stood two steps behind her, and his presence felt good.

It was still unbelievable to anyone who hadn't been paying attention. The dragnus had been injured and thrown back from the portal. The twins were somewhere on the other side, and it wasn't clear if they were still alive. Her hope was that they were dead and gone for good. As much as she wanted to consolidate power, she did not want to create heirs with either of them. No matter how much her father wanted the rest of the royal family to continue to have flight.

The portal had resisted letting anyone else through once the dragnus had been pushed back. Akeldama could only assume it had been the Traveler. Now it glowed a soft blue, and no one could make it through. That was a useful power. If only she had gotten more answers while the Traveler had been right here. Instead, the slaves had distracted her.

Demons streamed back through the portal without a problem. The king's anger was focused on them. They didn't stand a chance. They should have stayed and let the gargoyles kill them, for that would have been a quick and relatively painless death. The king was not so merciful.

Blood flew through the air as the royal guard watched the king's unadulterated rage. Bright red fire surrounded his claws as he swiped and tore into the deserters himself.

It took several minutes, but finally, he calmed down. It was a good thing, given how many lives they had lost between her brother's foolishness and now this. It would take decades to rebuild the demon population on this world. Not to mention the forces that had been pulled from other circles of hell.

When the portal at the other encampment had flickered blue and resisted all who tried to cross it, the king had assured her it was a fluke. He'd announced that the Traveler would need to stay there to maintain it. Now that it had happened again, and his watchers at the other camp said the other portal was still blocked, everyone saw it couldn't be a fluke. This could end his world campaigning. Akeldama could have told him about the third one, but he hadn't asked.

"Send troops to every portal off our worlds. Have them guarded!" His orders rippled through the crowd. The princess carefully turned her back to him and nodded at Typhon. They would gather her father's lieutenants and make a plan. It might not be the plan he would have chosen, but it would satisfy the order.

"Do it quickly," continued the king. "Keep them staffed with anyone who can fast travel. I want to know about any activity anywhere." The second round of the order caused her to pause and glance over her shoulder. She waited to see if any other orders were coming as the first two still rolled around inside of her chest.

The king moved closer to the dragnus, examining the wound on its snout. Red light flickered around the king's crown, a sign that he was controlling the dragnus. The creature's blood had stopped flowing over the rocks. An elven healer lay on the ground, passed out, completely covered in the red liquid.

"You will be fine," growled the king at the beast.

This wasn't the first time the princess had seen the king use the dragnus this way. She wasn't sure, but it seemed that the dragnus resisted the king at every turn. The history surrounding the great wyrm was unknown, and whenever she had dug into it, no one knew anything but myths and rumors. It was clear even when she was little that the king cared more about the dragnus than her or her brother. Not that it mattered anymore.

Once his attention was elsewhere, she continued on her way. It was time to make some plans. Maybe even contact a Traveler. If she could find one.

TWENTY-FOUR

Betha sat on the ground next to Angie's bedroll. Angie was in a deep sleep. At some point during the walk back to the camp, she had gone out like a light. Nessa had gotten her back and summoned the healer.

Eden was examining her now. Betha did her best to remain quiet and not interrupt the healer. She didn't want to get sent out of the tent.

"Can you explain what happened?" asked Eden.

"So, Angie is a shadow wolf," started Betha.

"Wait, what?" Eden glanced up from Angie.

"A shadow wolf—a type of shifter?"

Eden's eyes narrowed, and she set her hands back on Angie again. Her fingertips glowed bright white, then stopped.

"She doesn't feel like a shifter," muttered Eden. "Either way, her vitals have returned to normal, and she doesn't have any external wounds. Hopefully, sleep will do it. I need to get back to the medical tents. We have plenty of patients."

"Sorry for wasting your time," said Betha a bit acidly.

"I'm sorry, I didn't mean to be short," replied the angel. "This has just been a very difficult day for a healer. This wasn't a waste—her energy was all messed up and almost completely drained. I don't know how to explain it. The boost I gave her should be good enough to get her back on track. Let me know if she doesn't wake in a day or so."

Eden headed out of the tent. It was true. So many people were hurt. The trolls had taken the least amount of damage since they hadn't been able to fight in the sky, but even on the ground, it had been tough. The angels and the gargoyles, however, hadn't been spared at all. The demons had been prepared with arrows, spears, and other weapons to fight flying people. Thankfully, the trolls had been there, keeping the threats to the flyers mostly contained to other flyers. Still, many had died.

The portals each had Guardians. They had done it. Yet, it felt so incomplete. And Carter had kissed her, which was amazing, but also incomplete. Betha was confused on a lot of levels, but it felt like at least a partial victory.

"How is she doing?"

Betha glanced at the door and smiled at Carter. He was just within the doorway of the tent.

"Eden said she is doing okay and needs some rest now," she replied.

"How about we let her rest and we get you some food?" asked Carter.

Betha nodded and climbed to her feet. She gave Angie's hand a squeeze before she headed out. Carter led the way to the line where food was being served. The camp was quieter than before. Subdued. Angels flew overhead, keeping guard, though there weren't many demons left. Many people had bandages on some part of their body. When people spotted her, whether troll, gargoyle, or angel, they all gave her smiles and nods.

"We can grab some food and find somewhere quiet to eat," said Carter.

"Sounds good. I think food then sleep sounds just about right."

Once they received bowls of stew, Carter led her toward the edge of camp. Giant boulders rose up in the air. A pathway led to the top of a mound of rocks. It was much quieter here, above the noise and bustle, and Betha found the tension in her jaw vanishing. The sky was darkening quickly and the clouds from earlier were gone. They ate their stew in a comfortable silence as the stars came out.

"So, what's next? Are we going home?" asked Angie.

Betha leaned closer to her friend, clutching the thermos. All three of them were in the tent, sitting on the floor. "I don't know," Betha answered hesitantly.

"I promised Grandpappy that I would bring you back," answered Angie.

"I know, I know. It's just...I found another Traveler."

Both of her Anchors stared at her.

"It was when I vanished from the jail," Betha continued. She quickly summarized her experience with Genessa and the knife.

"I would say that sounds far-fetched, but then again, look where we are," said Carter. He motioned around the tent.

"So she's Kyra's grandmother? And Kyra fucked up?" asked Angie.

Betha shrugged and took a small sip of coffee. The smaller the sip, the longer it would last. "I don't know. I need to go back once you guys are safe. And to me, safe means back on Terra."

Carter leaned back on his arms. "Garruk and a few trolls will be heading that way soon. Most will stay here and help clean up the remaining demons, but he needs to report his findings to his people."

"You mean about Magnestial?" asked Angie.

"Yes, He plans to tell them everything."

If they headed back with the trolls, it would be a larger group. "I mean, that makes sense. We should go with them when they leave."

"Can I come in?" asked a deep voice at the door.

"Sure," answered Betha.

Sir Samson ducked into the doorway and smiled. Betha wondered what he thought. The group of them huddled together on the floor, with blankets piled high on Angie. She was still cold for some reason.

"I can't believe it is done. Rebuilding will take years, as will removing the last of the demons. Yet, there is hope. We have not had hope for many, many years. I thank each of you for this," said the tall gargoyle.

Betha quickly translated in her head for Angie and Carter since Sir Samson had spoken in his tongue.

"You are welcome," she replied, and meant it. It had been hard, harder than she had imagined in the council room so long ago, but it had been worth it. Now, there could again be little gargoyles, and they could rebuild their villages and their families.

"You must come visit Mountain Hold, I know Talli wanted to show you the records of the Starwalkers."

A giggle rose in Betha's chest. They had just decided that they were leaving, and now they were being invited to Mountain Hold. All she knew was that it was north, farther north than Rock Camp.

"How long would it take us to get there?" asked Carter.

"Only a few days' flying. You could see our city in the sky."

Betha glanced at Carter. "What about leaving with Garruk?"

Sir Samson interrupted. "They have at least a few days before they leave. Then they will need to travel overland back to the portal near Rock Camp. There is no reason you can't do both."

"Are you guys in?" asked Betha.

"You might need to see if I can take a sleeping potion, but why not," said Angie.

"We can't have come all the way here without actually seeing Mountain Hold," replied Carter.

"Sir Samson," said Betha, "it's a plan."

❧

Genessa didn't know what to make of this situation.

"You were banished from the nodes, any Traveler village, and contact with Travelers. Yet here you are?" Her voice was cold as she gazed down at the woman on the bed.

Andrea had white gauze wrapped around her shoulder, stopping the bleeding. Her eyes snapped wide open at the older woman's words. The room was dark, and slightly chilly from all of the surrounding rock.

"This is not possible." She struggled to get up, but her feet and hands had been bound to the bed. "I can't be here!"

"Didn't your visions warn you about coming here?" asked Genessa.

"I didn't mean to come here. *She* brought me here!"

Genessa shook her head and turned toward the doorway in the stone.

"You can't leave me here! I swear, it's not my fault! Don't leave me!"

Genessa didn't stop walking. The woman on the bed didn't deserve a response. Not after what she'd done. Still, it didn't explain Andrea showing up with the young Traveler, Betha. Even that had been forbidden—no contact with any Travelers. The commandment had been as clear as could be. All Travelers in this sector had been warned of the false seer.

As she stepped out into the sunshine, her eyes rose to the clouds. There had been too many riddles over the last couple of days, and it was clear Andrea had at some point been on Terra. Her thoughts flickered to her granddaughter. Maybe her failure hadn't been her own. It was easier for Genessa to believe Kyra had been misled than that she had really been so misguided.

"Poor Kyra. What did she do to you?"

The doorway behind her closed slowly, blocking out the light. Genessa turned to make sure it was secure. The prison cell looked like any other boulder. It would have to do for now, until she received some answers. Either way, Andrea would keep. She froze time inside the stone. The false seer wasn't going anywhere.

Betha would be along sooner or later, and then Genessa would get some of those answers. She hoped.

The Keeper of the Node went back to her hut where the kettle was just now starting to whistle.

Did you miss Traveler Forgotten? It's the story of the summer before Betha starts at St. Luna's! Sign up on my email list to get your copy!

TONI'S NOTES

We left Terra! Heading into the Feywilds is just the beginning for Betha and the gang. Exploring other worlds is a key part of this book, and the next one! Let your friends know what you think of the book. If you leave a review of the book, send it to me: toni@tonib-inns.com! I love to read reviews and feature them on my social media sites.

Are you wondering what happened to Eric? Don't worry - you will get his story, along with Susan's, in the Seer series. Not to mention a deeper look at what happened with him when Betha was traveling to the Heavens from book one. The Hidden Seer will be released in January, 2024.

Writing this book was fun! It feels like the characters kept pulling me in different directions, but in a good way. Courage of the Traveler kicks off right after this book ends, and we jump right back into things with Betha, Angie, and Carter. We finally get more information about the starwalkers, and the gargoyles. It was hard keeping my mouth shut, but so much comes out into the open in the next book! Courage will be released in October 2023.

To stay up to date join my newsletter: tonibinns.com

For book snippets, quotes and artwork check out my Instagram: @tonibinnsauthor